A
MAN
UNKNOWN

A MAN UNKNOWN

DEBBIE KING

A Man Unknown

iUniverse books may be ordered through booksellers or by contacting:

iUniverse
1663 Liberty Drive
Bloomington, IN 47403
www.iuniverse.com
1-800-Authors (1-800-288-4677)

Because of the dynamic nature of the Internet, any web addresses or links contained in this book may have changed since publication and may no longer be valid. The views expressed in this work are solely those of the author and do not necessarily reflect the views of the publisher, and the publisher hereby disclaims any responsibility for them.

Any people depicted in stock imagery provided by Thinkstock are models, and such images are being used for illustrative purposes only.
Certain stock imagery © Thinkstock.

ISBN: 978-1-4759-8600-6 (sc)
ISBN: 978-1-4759-8601-3 (e)

Print information available on the last page.

iUniverse rev. date: 01/04/2016

This book is dedicated in loving memory to my father, James Chapman.

Chapter One

Christmas Eve, such an exciting time, well at least it should be.

Christopher Walker and his eldest daughter, Michelle are both excitedly placing their presents under the tree, while waiting for their beloved Susan to arrive.

"Dashing through the snow," sings the radio as I drive to my father's house. The Christmas jingle ignites my excitement of this Christmas. This time last year I was in Switzerland, covering a huge story for my newspaper and therefore did not get to spend the festive season with my Father and Sister.

As I maneuver around the winding road, suddenly a bright light is in my eyes. It's completely blinding and I cannot see where I am going. "OH NO!" I yell as I realize I have no sense of direction and it also occurs to me, I'm not wearing my seat belt.

The car tumbles over the high ridge and I lose consciousness.

KNOCK, KNOCK, the doorknocker thuds against the heavy wooden front door. Christopher and Michelle almost run to welcome Susan. After what seems an eternity, she has finally arrived.

Opening the door wide, Christopher and Michelle are stunned to see two police officers standing before them.

"Mr. Walker, Mr. Christopher Walker?"

"Yes, that's right."

"WHAT'S WRONG?" Shrieks Michelle, as she grabs hold of her father.

"Mr. Walker, I'm very sorry but we believe your daughter, Susan has been involved in an accident. She is in the local hospital and we . . ."

"Immediately Officer, we're on our way," Christopher manages to intervene, nearly collapsing to the floor, as the weight of Michelle's frame becomes heavier from her sudden jelly legs.

"Would you like us to escort you Sir?"

"No . . . No . . . No thank you Officer, we'll travel together. What can we expect Officer?"

"All we can tell you Sir is that Susan needs to be positively identified and if the lady in hospital is indeed your daughter, the doctors will answer any questions you have."

"Why does she need identifying? Surely you know if it is her!"

"The lady driving the car was thrown from the wreck and her purse must have remained in the vehicle which exploded on impact. The car identification indicates the car was registered to Miss Susan Walker."

The drive to the hospital was deathly silent. Christopher just concentrating on his steering, Michelle looking out the window remembering the last time this exact drive was driven. It was almost twenty-two years ago, the day Susan was born. That drive was in excitement, but ended up tragic. Susan, Michelle's mother died while giving birth to her baby sister. Christopher named the baby in her mothers' memory. Michelle remembers looking down at that sweet baby girl who was born into an unloving world to face eternity without a mother. No she wouldn't, as Michelle decided at that very moment, not only would she be big sister, but she would treat this baby as her own. Looking out the window, not even the brightly lit Christmas lights of the house lined streets could bring a smile to Michelle's face. Michelle hated the hospital, as all she knew at this place was tragedy. Would tragedy strike in the same hospital tonight? Michelle couldn't bear the thought.

Walking into the hospital foyer made Michelle's heart race. What was she about to expect?

"Christopher Walker, I'm here to see my daughter."

"Right this way Mr. Walker."

As Christopher and Michelle enter the room, they see Susan lying in the hospital bed, asleep, with tubes attached to her beautiful face. The doctor monitoring her condition looks at Christopher. "Mr Walker, I'm Doctor Jenson, is this lady your daughter, Susan?"

"Yes it is her, what exactly is wrong with her?"

"She has some bruising to her body and face and has received a head injury"

"Exactly how bad is the injury?"

"There are no broken bones or internal damage to the body organs, but unfortunately Susan took a bump to her head and is in a coma."

Michelle let out an almighty scream at the news. Christopher embracing his daughter as her legs once again turn to jelly. "Michelle, take a seat," states Christopher, as he helps his daughter into a chair. "How long will Susan be in a coma for Doctor? Will she come out of it? Will she have brain damage?" Questions neither Christopher nor Michelle wanted to ask, but knew they must be answered.

"The answer to your questions cannot be answered just yet. Susan is very lucky to be alive. The tubes are to ensure Susan gets enough oxygen at the moment. We will do regular inspections of her lungs and they will be removed once her lungs are no longer in shock and are filling with enough oxygen to allow Susan to breathe on her own. That should be a couple of days at most. The best treatment for Susan is her family speaking to her daily. Love shown by family is the best medicine for coma patients."

"Yes, of course Doctor. We will stay with Susan for some time tonight and be here every day."

"Okay then, I'll leave you alone."

Chapter Two

Puzzled Michelle drives from Los Angeles to Pasadena to find out the reason she has been called into the Pasadena Police Department. It's been a whole month since the accident, why would the police contact her after so long? Of course, being a Detective she has suspicions but hesitates to jump to conclusions. Better wait until the discussion with Detective Oliver.

Michelle pulls up her black BMW outside the Pasadena Police Department. She walks to the front desk, showing her Los Angeles Detective badge and asks to speak with Detective Oliver in charge of Susan's accident investigation. Inside the sound proof glass office the investigation begins. The investigation reveals that the police believe Susan's car has been tampered with, causing the car to explode on impact. An attempted murder investigation is under way.

"So Detective Walker, is there anyone you can think of who would want Susan dead?"

"No!"

"Did she have any enemies that you know of?"

"No" . . . "As Susan's sister I want full participation in the investigation."

"Sorry Detective, but as you already know, you cannot be involved in the investigation, due to conflict of interest."

"Stuff conflict of interest, I WANT IN!"

"No can do, sorry."

"Look being my sister I want immediate details given to me, whatever you find, okay?"

"Okay Detective but that's all I can do, you cannot be part of the investigation."

"So do you have any leads, a starting point?"

"All we know at the moment is the fuel tank had a small hole drilled into it, enough to cause a leak, which in turn caused the explosion."

"Have you spoken to my father about this yet?"

"No I haven't. I thought because you are a detective I would discuss this with you first."

"Well, leave it between you and me. With Dad's health I'd rather he not know anything about this!"

"Okay Detective, you have my word. Although it would be necessary to talk to him to find out if he knows of anyone who may have cause to kill Susan."

"Leave it with me, I'll talk to him. Thank you for your time, stay in touch."

With heated anger Michelle heads to the hospital. Susan is still in a coma. All tubes have been removed and she is breathing on her own now. Improvement, but unfortunately not enough. "Oh Susan, what happened? Please baby wake up, I need you, I miss you, I love you." Susan remains asleep, no signs of life other than the faint depression of her chest as she breathes. Michelle stays for some time, holding Susan's hand. The memories come flooding back of Susan's childhood. The very day she was born she was taken home and her father hired a nurse until she was declared well enough to be cared for by a nanny. How Michelle adored Susan. She meant the world to her and amazingly she grew to look like her name sake. Looking down at Susan, Michelle focuses on her beauty. Her beautiful dark wavy hair surrounding her model face. Her cherry red full lips, perfectly straight nose and her olive flawless skin, her big eyes, even closed and bruised seem to radiate beauty. Strange, here is Susan a model of perfection and yet so humble. How often had Susan told Michelle she hoped to grow as beautiful as she? So many times Michelle can't remember.

"Maybe the kiss of true love can wake her," states Matthew as he enters the room.

"Oh Matthew if only that were true, but only in the fairy tales."

Matthew and Susan have been dating for just over a year now. "So Matthew have all your and Susan's friends now been notified of Susan's accident?"

"Yes as far as I know, why's that?"

"No reason, other than I want Susan to have as much support and visitors as possible to help her come out of the coma. Anyway I've been here for quite some time, so I'll leave you with her." Michelle bends over Susan kissing her on the forehead, bids Matthew farewell and leaves the room.

Driving to her father's estate, Michelle thinks of all the friends who have visited Susan. No one of suspicion comes to mind. They all love Susan and they all seem sincere. Still Michelle makes a mental note to supply Detective Oliver with all their names. Christopher is sitting in front of the fire enjoying the warmth. "Hi Dad."

"Michelle, how are you darling? Have you just come from seeing your sister?

"Yes. Still no change."

"Hmm."

Michelle sits in the leather recliner next to her father. Staring at the flames in the fireplace, Michelle thinks of a way to approach the subject of Susan having any enemies. Michelle realizes this is no easy task to succeed without her father becoming suspicious. "Dad, do you think we have remembered everyone who knows Susan to inform them of her condition?"

"Yes love, I think so."

"Even from our childhood?"

"Yes, I'm quite sure. Besides if we've forgotten anybody they have probably read about it in the paper by now."

Of course, how stupid thinks Michelle. Of course it would be in all the major papers, especially since Susan is a journalist. It occurs to Michelle that whoever wanted Susan dead would know that she actually isn't. Is her life still in danger? Michelle decides to start her own private investigation from her department in Los Angeles. What Detective Oliver doesn't know won't hurt him. Father and daughter sit in silence, somehow realizing that saying nothing at all and just being together is all the comfort they need. Time has a way of passing unnoticed and before they realize it, it is dark outside. They share the evening meal together and then Michelle heads home to Los Angeles.

Chapter Three

Susan's eyelids begin to wave. She hears strange sounds. She opens her eyes. "Where am I?"

"Susan, you had an accident and you're in the hospital," responds the nurse.

"An accident, how, when?"

"Can you remember anything at all?"

"I remember who I am and the last thing I remember was driving to my father's for Christmas."

"That's right, but you didn't make it to your dad's. You're lucky to be alive."

"What time is it, nurse?"

"It's 12.35."

"Oh, okay, well don't disturb my father or Michelle now, just leave them sleep and contact them first thing in the morning."

"Okay, I'll just notify the doctor now that you're awake." The nurse leaves the room. Susan closes her eyes once again.

"Susan, I'm Doctor Edwards. How are you feeling?"

"I feel fine, but is it okay to turn the light on so I can see you, or will I disturb other patients?"

"Susan, it's 12.50 in the afternoon, the curtains are open, the sun is shining and you are in a room by yourself. Can you not see me?"

"NO, NO I CAN'T." The realization of no sight terrifies Susan into a panic attack.

"Calm down Susan. We'll run some tests and see what's going on with your sight. But in the meantime we'll ring your father and tell him you're awake."

Christopher arrives to Susan in tears. As he tries in vain to comfort his daughter, Susan just becomes more upset with the knowledge she may never see again. Christopher stays by her bedside and waits for Michelle to arrive.

Doctor Edwards calls for the Ophthalmologists, Doctor Richards. "Susan, I'm Doctor Richards and I specialize in eyes and sight. I will carry out some tests and find out exactly what is wrong and if the blindness is permanent."

"So the blindness may not be permanent Doctor?" enquires Christopher.

"No, not always! Depending on where the damage is and the severity, sometimes surgery can be performed and the eyes can regain sight after some weeks. But I won't know until the tests results are in."

Michelle arrives and when she sees her father comforting Susan, realizations hits that even though Susan has awakened from her coma, all is not well. Christopher relates to Michelle all that the Doctor has stated. All they can do now is await the test results. With nothing else they can do Christopher and Michelle leave.

Ring, Ring, it's the telephone. Christopher picks up the handset; "Mr Walker, It's Doctor Richards. Susan's test results are in and I would like for you, Michelle and Matthew to be present when I reveal the results to Susan."

"What's wrong Doc, are the results good or bad?"

"I cannot reveal that information over the phone, sorry Mr Walker, but all will be revealed when you all arrive."

"Ok Doctor, we'll see you soon."

At the hospital, everyone eagerly awaits for Doctor Richards to reveal the test results. "Susan, the results are in and I'm sorry to tell you, but they are not good." The room is eerily quiet; faces appear statue like as the family stare at Doctor Richards. "Just how bad is the result, Doctor?" Enquires Christopher.

"With the combination of Susan hitting the back of her head as well as the bump around her eyes, the injury has caused permanent damage. Susan's eyesight will never be any better than it is now."

"But why, exactly why can't an operation help?" Demands Christopher.

Doctor Richards produces a chart with a picture of the brain, as he explains in detail the reason why. "The brain has a region called the occipital cortex, this area of Susan's brain has been damaged so badly when she hit her head, that it cannot be repaired and she will not even have light perception anymore." The family listen intently as the realization that Susan's life will forever be changed is almost too much to bear, both girls break down crying intensely. Christopher comforts Michelle as Matthew comforts Susan. After some time the girls settle down and the family discuss the situation. "Looks like I'll have to give up my journalism career," states Susan. No reply. Just what does one say to such a statement?

"Can I please have a moment with Susan alone?" Asks Matthew. Michelle, Christopher and Dr Richard leave the room. "Susan, I'm so sorry to hear of your outcome, but I must be totally honest with you."

"What are you talking about?"

"Susan because you will be blind forever I'm sorry to say but I won't be able to continue our relationship."

Susan yells "What do you mean you're sorry. Why, why does this have to end our relationship?"

Christopher bursts open the door upon hearing his daughter yell. "Leave at once and never come near my family again." Matthew walks out the door, as Susan breaks down uncontrollably. "Why Dad, why would he do this to me?"

"I don't know Susan, but if that is his attitude he can go to hell."

"I'll never be able to be loved again because of my blindness, Dad. No one will ever accept me."

"Now now Susan, let's not jump to conclusions. Let's concentrate on getting you home and learn to live and cope with your condition first and we'll worry about that when the need arises."

"Well that's never going to arise, anyway how am I going to live on my own?'

"Well you won't have to. You can come live with me." With that issue settled, Susan continues to be upset, but manages to put on a brave front at the same time.

The Doctor discusses with the family how the rehabilitation program will commence and works out a possible date for Susan to go live at her fathers.

Chapter Four

few weeks pass and Susan has now learnt how to walk with a cane and feel confident. It's time to go home. Christopher drives his daughter back to their mansion, which actually has the appearance of an eighteen hundreds castle. Once inside the castle, Susan realizes she doesn't need her cane to guide her steps. Her memory of walking in this house all her life is as if she can see once more. How much better this makes her feel. It's so good to be in familiar surroundings. The maid takes Susan's bag and proceeds upstairs to her bedroom to put her things away for her.

Susan, her father and Michelle all just take in the moment they thought would never happen. The Christmas tree still stands with unopened presents underneath. Together the family enjoy a very belated celebration. Once the Christmas celebration is over, Christopher produces a bottle of wine and three wine glasses for a special celebration, a celebration of the life of his daughter. Together the three get very tipsy and after hours of talking and reminiscing they head to bed.

A new day, a new life. Today Susan starts her adult life all over again. The day begins as normal but one exception, Christopher gives Susan another gift. "I thought all the present opening occurred last night," states Susan.

"All the Christmas presents yes, but this is a special gift for your new life." Susan takes the present and opens the box. Feeling the gift she can sense it is a laptop. "How am I ever going to be able to use this Dad?"

"I had the guys in the factory invent a computer especially for you. It is one hundred per cent voice activated and instead of a touch pad it has a fingerprint reader so you can lock the laptop and no one else can have access to it. It also has a one piece head phone so you can hear what you are researching as well as listen to the environment around you, so you know when someone is talking to you."

"Oh Dad, thank you so much. It's just wonderful. I'll at least be able to stay up to date with the world and current affairs," Susan states, not realizing her inner journalist sub-conscious mind is at play. Susan proceeds to open the laptop and Christopher helps her to set it up for operation.

Michelle gets ready to head back to Los Angeles to continue her investigation of a well-known Lawyer's home which was burnt down, killing both him and his wife. "Well, I'm off. I've got an arson case to investigate. Will visit as soon as I can."

After forensic investigation, it is believed that the Home was deliberately lit. The department believe an arsonist is operating in the city. "Now that I have a laptop I can use, if there is anything I can research or anyone I can contact with my journalist contacts to help the investigation, just let me know," states Susan.

"Will do Sis, but I think you have enough to worry about."

"Oh come on Shell, please? It'll give me something to worry about other than myself."

"Ok, if you insist. I don't think you'll be able to discover much though; all major leads have been investigated and exhausted. We really don't know where to turn to next."

"All right, but if I manage to dig something up, I'll let you know. Now come give your little sister a hug goodbye." The two sisters embrace and Michelle leaves.

Susan immediately opens her laptop and starts investigating the fire. The Lawyer and his wife who died in their own home were Peter and Shirley Bradford. Their only son Joseph was away on holiday in the Bahamas at the time of the fire, thus he is in the clear. Susan searches for a connection between the fire and Joseph. Nothing. She closes the laptop and leaves it for now. She decides to contact some of her old work colleagues back in Los Angeles to ask what, if any advancements have developed in the news on the fire. No results there either. Nothing but dead ends.

Christopher asks his daughter to join him for a picnic in their Mansion grounds. Susan agrees and the two stroll out to the beautiful surroundings. Susan's memory of the gardens and the acreage are so vivid, it's as if she can see the trees and flowers, as she takes in their beautiful aroma. During the picnic, Susan asks her father can she buy a guide dog as not only a help but for companionship as well. The picnic finishes and they walk back to the house and ring the foundation for the blind to organize a dog.

Christopher and Susan arrive at the guide dog for the blind facility and Susan acquaints herself with the dogs. She picks out a female Labrador that really seems to love Susan already. Her name is Molly.

Chapter Five

A few months have passed since Susan has bought her dog. The two have formed a close bond. The day is sunny and Susan decides to go for a walk in the estate grounds. She heads out front. Susan and Molly enjoy their time together in the grounds as Susan takes in all the sounds and aromas in the air of the grass, trees and flowers. The two have been doing this every day for some time now.

On the road in front of the castle an Audi is broken down. A man gets out of the vehicle to look under the hood. Not being of mechanical mind he decides to call for help. Searching for his cell phone he realizes he has left it behind. He looks around and spots the castle some meters off the road. Hoping someone is home and friendly at that, he walks the driveway. On the way up he hears a dog playfully barking. He stops to watch. He can't believe his eyes when he sees before him the most beautiful woman he can recall ever seeing. He stands beneath a huge tree just watching, mesmerized by the woman's beauty. Without realizing, he accidently steps on a fallen twig. SNAP. Immediately Molly runs towards him and Susan asks "Who's there?"

"Sorry to frighten you, my name is Steven Sheppard. My car broke down and I've left my cell phone at home and cannot call for help. I'm walking up to the castle to ask if I can use the telephone."

"Oh, well firstly hi, my name is Susan and I live in that castle, with my father. If you walk with me, I'll gladly allow you to use the phone."

"Thank you madam, it's so kind of you. I feel like such a fool leaving my cell behind."

"Well we all forget things at times, don't worry about it." Together the two and the dog walk to the castle. Upon seeing the castle, Steven is in awe. "Wow, I can't believe you actually live in a castle."

"Have done my whole life, so I'm used to it."

"It must make you feel like a princess."

"I wish. No, only like the princess locked in the castle tower waiting for Prince Charming to come rescue me."

"Whatever do you mean?"

"Well with me being blind, who would ever want me? I'll be here forever and a day."

"I don't see how you being blind has anything to do with being single your entire life." With those words, they reach the front door; end of conversation. As they enter the building, Christopher jumps to his feet. "Dad, this is Steven and he just needs to use our phone as his car broke down."

"Mr Walker, nice to meet you," states Christopher.

"Thank you for your kind hospitality, Sir," replies Steven, as the two men shake hands. Christopher leads Steven to the telephone and Steven makes the call. As Steven calls, he can't take his eyes off of Susan. Nothing gets past Christopher, when it comes to his protective shield he has developed for his daughter. He notices Steven's stare and smile on his face as he looks upon his daughter. Maybe an opportunity has arisen for Susan to acquaint herself with this man. Christopher decides to jump at the window of opportunity, before the window closes. "So, what will happen with your car, young man?"

"Sounds as if a tow truck is coming to take the vehicle to a garage to be repaired." Christopher demands "I'll drive you back to your car to help with the loading."

"Thank you Sir that is most kind."

"How will you be getting home then Steven?"

"Well, if I may use the phone again, Sir I'll call for a cab."

"No need for that, I'll drive you," states Christopher, not wanting to miss time to speak with and get to know this man a bit better.

"Are you sure, Sir?"

"Absolutely, I insist."

"Ok, thank you kind Sir." With that, the two leave Susan to go to Steven's car. The drive down the driveway is quiet. But while waiting for the tow truck to arrive, Christopher starts a conversation. "I couldn't help but notice how much you were looking at my daughter while you were on the phone.'"

"Yes Sir"

"Well? Why is that?" Asks Christopher, already knowing the answer.

"Well as you would well know, Sir, she is extremely beautiful."

"Yes, that's right, she is beautiful, but she is also completely blind."

"Yes, I know Sir."

"And that doesn't bother you?"

"What do you mean, Sir?"

"Well, I know what a man is thinking when he looks at a woman the way you were looking at my daughter. I've only ever looked at one woman that way and she became my wife and mother to my two beautiful daughters."

"Sir, just what are you implying?"

"I'm not implying anything; I'm just asking does it bother you if she is blind?"

"No Sir, not at all."

"Good." Good. What does he mean by good wonders Steven? Is Mr Walker trying to get his daughter a man to date? The tow truck arrives and Steven hands over his keys. Christopher and Steven get into Christopher's car and Steven knows this is going to be an interesting drive back to his place. Just as Steven suspected, the drive back to his place is full of questions.

"So, Steven, how old are you?"

"I'm thirty three."

"I notice you don't wear a ring, are you married?"

"No."

"Any children, ex-wife?"

"No Sir, never been married, never have had children."

"Do you plan on marriage?"

"One day Sir, when I meet the right one and I fall in love." Strange questions.

"So you're single then?"

"At the moment, yes."

"Hmm. Work, what do you do for work?"

"I am a pilot, so I am away a lot, of course."

"So why were you out our way?"

"I was going for a drive in the country to have a look." Gee such personal questions

"A look at what exactly?"

"Just looking, thought I'd like to buy a house in the country, so just checking out this area." Has this man ever heard of minding his own business?

"Hmm."

As Steven opens his door to exit the car, he is asked yet another question. "Steven, before you leave, would you like to come to our place for dinner Friday night?"

Hesitating to answer after the experience with this man, Steven thoughts turn to the beautiful Susan. "Only if Susan will be there sir, no offense!"

"No offence taken, see you at six pm sharp."

"Ok Sir, thank you for the drive home," Steven says as opening his wallet to offer some fuel money.

"Put that a way, it's been my pleasure."

I bet it has been with the interrogation I just received thinks Steven. The two men shake hands and with that Christopher drives off leaving Steven on the footpath. I'm amazed he didn't want to inspect the house, Steven thinks to himself.

Chapter Six

Friday evening arrives and Steven arrives at the castle. Walking up the stairs to the front door, Steven can't help but wonder what sort of night he is in for with Christopher around. He knocks on the door, using the huge door knocker hanging on the impressive door. The maid opens and takes Steven's jacket, then directs him to the dining room. For the first time Steven takes a good look at the interior of the castle. It's quite impressive, almost unbelievable. The foyer, the study he walked past and now the dining room. Every room is huge, beautifully decorated with antiques, a fortune the place is worth a fortune. Steven looks upon the biggest dining table he has ever seen, adorned with silver, flowers and candles. Already sitting at the head end is of course Christopher, with Susan to his left. The maid offers Steven the seat to Christopher's right and opposite Susan. "Welcome Steven," announces Christopher. Steven sits, feeling uneasy with the situation at hand. He wonders will he impress Christopher? At least he doesn't have to worry about what Susan sees; he'll just have to watch how he speaks. He is pleased he chose to wear a black dinner suit and tie.

As the entree is served, Steven watches Christopher and his daughter to make sure he mimic's each step of proper table etiquette to just about perfection. Never having eaten in such company, makes Steven nervous and he fumbles with minor things. As the last mouthful of the main course enters Steven's mouth, he drops his fork, narrowly missing the expensive china plate. "You seem edgy Steven, is there a reason for this?" Enquires Christopher.

"Well Sir, It's just that I've never eaten at a table so formal in my life, with such delicate crockery."

"Hmm," the same usual reply from Christopher. Steven can't help but wonder what's with all the hmming this man does. All throughout the three courses, not another word is spoken. Weird thinks Steven, too frightened to make the first attempt at speaking. Once the meal is complete, Christopher invites Steven into the sitting room for conversation. Susan joins them.

The sitting room is huge with a marble top bar at one end and an elaborate fireplace at the other. In the center of the room are two leather recliners and two, two seater sofas, also leather. White leather to match the marble floor, bar top and fireplace mantelpiece. The room is painted a brilliant baby blue, making for a stunning effect. A huge baby blue rug separates the sofas. On the walls are huge family portraits. A beautiful portrait of Christopher, his deceased wife and a young girl, most probably Michelle. Susan looks exactly like her Mother. A true beauty.

"Would you like a drink, Steven?"

"Scotch please." Christopher pours three drinks and gives one to each. Steven notices suddenly there are no servants in the room. Shakily Steven takes his Scotch. "Settle my boy, there is no need for nerves; we're just going to have a chat." Steven worries that Susan knows how nervous he is with what her father has to say. Anyway she would be able to hear the ice trembling in the glass. Why do I have ice? I didn't ask for ice Steven thinks to himself.

"Susan, Darling, Steven tells me he's a pilot."

"Really, that must be most interesting to travel the globe?"

"Yes quite, an important but exciting occupation," answers Steven.

"Also involves a little bit of danger," remarks Susan. Susan secretly smiles from within, as she loves a man of danger. This aspect of Steven's life intrigues her. She hopes to get to know this man better. But how? "Yes I suppose there is some danger involved in flying, but no more than there is in driving on the roads."

"Hmm," mutters Christopher. There it is again, that hmm, seriously what is it with this man and his hmming? "So is it just airplanes you fly or can you fly helicopters as well?" Christopher inquires.

"Just planes, no choppers Sir."

"Hmm, that's a pity. I would have invited you to take Susan and I for a joy flight in my helicopter." Christopher owns his own private chopper, just how wealthy is this man? "Well, tell me Steven, apart from flying and driving broken down cars, what else do you do?" Did my father actually just say those words to Steven? How humiliating!

"I do enjoy fishing." Fishing, not exactly up Susan's alley.

"How about horse riding?"

"Never ridden a horse in my life, Sir."

"Well then, no time like the present to start."

"Daddy!" Susan blurts out, quite shocked at her father's boldness.

"Hush dear. So Steven how about it are you up for learning to ride?" Trying extremely hard not to show any sign of fear, Steven responds with "Yes Sir, I'll be willing to give it a try."

"Good! Susan loves to ride, so when is your next time off?

"Daddy, what are you implying? I can't go riding. I haven't been on a horse for about four years now, not to mention I can't see where I'm riding," interrupts Susan; sounding quite worried herself at the aspect of riding blind.

"Hush dear. You will still be able to ride, once you have the ability, you never lose it. So Steven when are those days you have off and you and Susan can go riding?"

"Obviously Sir, It's quite clear that Susan isn't comfortable with that, so therefore I'd better decline the offer." Suddenly Steven felt some relief. He and animals do not go well together. "Nonsense! Susan will be alright, she's ridden since she could walk."

"But Sir, if Susan is not comfortable without being able to see while riding, I wouldn't like to force her hand and make her feel obligated to do so just for me."

"Are you that scared you are trying to find an excuse not to ride, Steven?"

"No Sir, not at all. But if Susan isn't ready to try riding again just yet, maybe a future time would be better."

"Daddy, Please?"

"Hush dear! Steven when are those days off?"

"Not to be rude Sir, but I really would rather not force Susan. I know I would not like to fly blind."

"Fly blind? Why you must do that all the time, surely?"

"Yes Sir, I do indeed fly blind so to speak, but I always have the control panel with the exact reading of my location. Horse riding must be completely different."

"Not really, Susan has the reins and the horse isn't stupid, he knows where to tread." Really not having an answer to this, Steven surrenders. "I work the next week and have four days off starting on the Wednesday."

"Good, it's settled, be here at eight am sharp. You'll join us for breakfast and then the fun can begin."

"Yes Sir! I thank you and Susan for your hospitality and bid you farewell."

"Good night Steven." Both Christopher and Susan say together. Christopher rings a bell and the maidservant enters the room. "Please get Steven's jacket and escort him to his car." With that the two men shake hands and Steven leaves the home.

Susan with a scowl on her face gives her father a kiss good night and heads to bed. Never has Susan seen this controlling personality trait in her father. She is definite she does not like it though.

The next morning Christopher and Susan enjoy breakfast on the front veranda, soaking up the sunshine. Susan cannot contain her silence any longer. "So Father, why were you so demanding on Steven last night?"

"Just looking after your best interest, dear!"

"Looking after my best interest? It was obvious he didn't want to come here for the day."

"Nonsense, he just doesn't want to learn to ride a horse."

"Ride a horse? Daddy; you're practically forcing him to do so. I don't see why it's so important to you for him to do so."

"Like I said, just looking after your best interest."

"And like I said, he clearly doesn't want to come here!"

"Yes he does, as much as you want him to come here again. Just had to think of an activity you can both do." Susan is totally shocked at how stern her father is speaking.

"Daddy, I've never known you to be so forceful before. It scares me!"

"No darling, it's nothing to worry about; I just have to act on your behalf, since you obviously like this fellow but are too shy to do anything about it yourself."

"Just how do you know I like him, Daddy?"

"Body language dear, body language." Susan lets out a coy giggle. "See that's exactly what I'm talking about." Christopher stands up and embraces Susan with a cuddle. "Anyway darling, its better we get to know this man on our property."

Without realizing it Susan responds with "Thank you so much Dad;" followed by the same coy giggle. With that they both go about their days activities.

Chapter Seven

It's Friday and Michelle has a busy day ahead of her, chasing down leads to the arson case. Without breakfast, she jumps into her car with her partner and heads for the crime scene. On the way a vehicle catches her eye; it's her father's Volvo. It's parked outside of a church called 'Belief Church'. "Strange name for a church;" states Michelle's partner.

"Sure is," answers Michelle, meanwhile thinking its much stranger that her father's car is out the front so early in the morning. Why would that be? She decides she will discuss this with her father when she sees him. "Doesn't everyone who goes to church have a belief?"

The crime scene lets out no secrets. Forensics have discovered there was a slow gas leak in the pipes which is what caused the fire. But a naked flame had to be within the leakage or the house wouldn't ignite on its own. Time to question the neighbors some more. Last time the neighbors were questioned no-one saw anything. Door after door, the same response. Knocking on a door about six houses away and on the opposite side of the road, a teenage girl answers the door. "Detective Walker and Detective Jones," says Michelle while showing her badge. "Just investigating the fire down the road, you didn't happen to see anything that night, did you, Miss?"

"Actually I did."

"You did? Exactly what did you see? Miss umm?"

"Lola, the names Lola. Yes I did see something that night."

"Why weren't we told earlier, we've already questioned this neighborhood?" Asks Detective Jones.

"Sorry Officers, it's only Mum and Dad who were questioned, not me."

"Well why didn't you speak up?" Demands Detective Jones. Lola is looking quite scared by this point and Michelle's protective nature takes over.

"I'll handle this Jones!" States Michelle, being the senior of the two and knowing how to deal appropriately with young girls. "It's okay Lola. How old are you?"

"Sixteen, Detective."

"Call me Michelle and my friend here is Donna. So you're sixteen and you didn't get asked any questions the first time we called around? Is that right?"

"Yes! That's right. Mum and Dad were home and said we didn't see anything, but they didn't know I did. No-one's going to be in trouble, are they Michelle?"

"No, no, it's okay. Just tell us what you know and why you didn't tell us sooner."

"I was too scared to say anything, because I snuck out that night to meet my boyfriend and when I saw the fire, I snuck back inside and hid my boyfriend in my cupboard. You see Mum and Dad both thought I was asleep when the explosion took place. It's the first time I snuck out and I haven't done it since."

"I see," says Michelle, remembering what it was like to be sixteen and think you love the guy from school. "What exactly did you see, Lola?"

"Well I just got on the ground and I saw a man running past our house opposite side of the street."

"What was he wearing, any distinguishing marks? Tattoos, anything like that?"

"Well I only had the glare of the flames and the street light. All I saw was he was nearly bald, had his hair really short. But I remember thinking he looked around thirty and about the same height as my Dad."

"How tall is your Dad?"

"Six foot."

"What clothes was he wearing?"

"He had on a track suit, a dark color, either navy or black."

"Which direction was he running?"

"That way, away from the fire."

"So he wasn't running to help with the fire?"

"Didn't look like it."

"Thanks Lola, you've helped us lots today."

"Please don't tell my Mum and Dad, Michelle. I'll be in trouble."

"I won't say anything yet Lola, but we need to report this information and hopefully it helps us catch whoever did this. You may have to give a testimony in court, so your parents could eventually find out. Do you have your own cell?"

"Yes."

"I'll tell you what; since you were so informative and have given us a lead, I'll take your number and talk with you if we need you further. You will have to come to the station and give a statement."

"Can I do that now?"

"Shouldn't you be getting to school?"

"No I have today off, girls' problems. Today would be good."

"Okay, let's go."

Success at last! Maybe with this information, we can find the killer, thinks Michelle. Lola makes her statement and is driven home again, grateful that her parents don't have to be informed just yet. At the end of the day, Michelle calls her father to ask when she can visit next. "Wednesday morning, Susan has a gentleman joining us for breakfast and then going horse riding. It would be good if you could join us."

"I have Tuesday and Wednesday off, so I can sleep over if you'd like."

"Of course Darling."

"How has Susan got herself a date, who is this man?"

"Enough with the detective work. You will meet him when he comes for the day. Trust me, he is a nice young man."

"Okay Daddy," submits Michelle, secretly knowing not only is her detective at work here, but so is her motherly protection for Susan. Oh no, did I do the right thing with Lola?

Chapter Eight

Tuesday arrives and Michelle heads to her fathers. On arrival all Michelle can do is question her father and Susan about this 'gentleman' as her father put it. "So Daddy, just who is this man coming to see Susan for the day? Susan how did you get to meet a man, not on the web I hope?"

"Whoa, one question at a time, you've only just arrived. Go unpack your things first and then we'll talk." The maid servant knows she is not to touch Michelle's things; after all she may well have her pistol or Taser with her. Michelle does as her father says.

Michelle looks around her room; impressed with the way her father left it exactly how she'd left it. Out dated, that's what it is; time for some new décor. I mean honestly who can sleep with pictures of high school guys, singers and actors one thought was all but when one was seventeen when one is now twenty-nine? Michelle takes the time to tear down all the posters on the wall. Just blank rectangles and squares were they hung and the paint didn't fade due to their being there. Michelle has stayed in this room every time she sleeps over. Why has it just bothered her now how it looks? Is it because of the fire and Lola, or the suspense over her sister and this man? Michelle isn't sure; but she is sure she's glad she has gotten rid of them. Man, her father and his ways. Michelle wonders what Susan must think of seeing this demanding side of him. Michelle has always known it existed, but not Susan; she has never had to witness this before. Michelle walks over to her window, which faces the back of the property and takes a look outside. Looking down at the huge in ground pool and court yard, nothing has changed there either. The land still looks the same too, all beautifully manicured. The gardener does a great job. Walking into the bathroom, Michelle checks for supplies and as usual, her father has it well maintained for her. Beautiful fresh smelling towels and washers, new soap and toiletries. Michelle loves how prepared her father makes everything for her; well at how he makes his maid servants do so.

Heading back down the spiral staircase, Michelle notices her father enter his library and close the door. She decides to leave him alone. She remembers how as a child her father often would go into his library and spend quite some time alone in there. Why was that? Did he love reading that much? Why was it his library, why not the family's library? Why have two libraries in the house? Strange; her father can be a strange man. Walking out onto the front veranda, Michelle sees Susan swing back and forth in the swing chair. "Mind if I join you?"

"Of course not, come; sit." Michelle takes a seat beside her sister. It's a good time to investigate this man. No point beating about the bush, just get straight into it. "So Susan, you seem quite happy now."

"Yes a lot happier than the last time you saw me."

"That's good. Is it because of this man?"

"Well he is part of the reason, but now I have Molly and I'm comfortable and learning to live a blind life isn't so bad."

"So, who is this man? I don't even know his name; calling him 'this man', is not a good thing."

"His name is Steven and Daddy tells me he is thirty-three."

"Thirty-three! Isn't he just a bit old for you Sis?"

"Daddy doesn't think so. I mean look at Daddy. Mum was younger than him by ten years; what's two more years? Not much really."

"Yeah, I suppose when you put it like that; it doesn't seem too bad."

"How did you meet him, was it on one of your outings?"

"No. . ."

"Oh, please don't tell me it was on the net?" Interrupts Michelle

"No it wasn't on the net. His car broke down and he used our phone."

"You're having a date with a man you met while using our house phone?"

"Well Daddy organized it; not Steven or myself." Of course he did, thinks Michelle.

"Michelle, can you please tell me what he looks like?"

"Of course I will."

The two girls decide to go for a swim. When they get out, Christopher emerges from his library. "Honestly Daddy; what do you do in your library for so long?" Enquires Michelle.

"Well; it is a place for reading and alone quiet time, which I like." Answers Christopher whilst giving his daughter a stern look as if she has no right to enquire. Michelle takes the hint and lets the subject drop. Gee; touchy. How come it's the only room in the house without a surveillance camera? Other than bedrooms and bathrooms that is. But all other public areas have cameras, including the other library; why not this library? Is it such a secret that the door must be locked and no-one can see within the room. Plus Christopher is the only one with the key. Michelle decides she must investigate this.

The afternoon is spent with the sisters discussing how Michelle should have her room revamped. Michelle decides on purple and Susan also decides to revamp her bedroom and as yellow is her favorite color, she gets Michelle to choose a lovely yellow and decides on white trimmings. All set, they approach their father for the permission to do so. Of course the permission is granted and they also choose to rip up the carpets and have timber flooring. Christopher immediately calls a carpenter to start the work. The family decide to go to a restaurant for dinner and gives the maid servant the night off. Returning from dinner, everyone is exhausted and heads straight to their rooms to retire for the night. Tomorrow is going to be a big day.

Eight am sharp and Steven pounds on the front door. "Punctuality, I like that in a man," states Christopher, "A man who is punctual, is usually a man you can trust." Christopher extends his hand to shake. Steven accepts. "Firm hand shake, I like that too." Christopher takes Steven into the house into the huge dining room, where not only is the beautiful Susan sitting, but also another beautiful woman. "Steven; I'd like you to meet my eldest daughter, Michelle." Michelle extends her hand and Steven lifts it to his lips and gently kisses the back of her hand. Is this guy for real; who does this these days? "Please be seated," Christopher's voice dominates the room. All sit. Breakfast consists of a smorgasbord. Hotcakes, toast, spread, baked beans, sausages, bacon, eggs, cereal, fruit, tea, coffee, milk and juice all spread on the table. Steven decides to steer clear of baked beans, in case of any after effects; especially if horse riding for the first time today. With a full stomach, Christopher decides they are to wait three quarters of an hour for the food to settle before they ride. Now this decision pleases Steven. Michelle and Susan leave the room to get Susan dressed into her jodhpurs, ready for riding. Susan is nervous, but has at least had some time to ride while waiting for this day to arrive. With anticipation Susan can't wait any longer. "So Shell, what's he look like? Is he good looking?"

"Well Sis, when you go riding together today why don't you feel his face and describe him to me later and I'll see how well your touch is working."

"Aww, come on tell me now."

"No, I want you to describe him. It'll be more fun that way." Susan, knowing how stubborn her sister is doesn't push the subject any further. "Okay, okay; I just don't know how to achieve such a challenge."

"I'm sure you'll think of a way." With that the sisters walk back down the stairs.

"Well now Steven, my good man take my daughter and enjoy your horse riding." Steven takes Susan nervously by the arm and Molly immediately tags along as Susan leads the way to the stables.

At the stables, the stable hand leads out two very quiet horses and hands Susan her reins. Susan mounts her horse, as Steven stands dumbfounded. The stable hand immediately goes to assist Steven. "Always mount and dismount the horse from the left side." Steven takes the reins and puts his left foot into the stirrup and climbs into the saddle. Reins in hand Steven is very scared. The stable hand leads the horses to the paddock especially prepared for Susan to ride blind. No trees, just mowed green grass fenced by plastic look alike wood posts and railings, painted white. Once in the paddock, Susan takes the lead; only walking the horse, realizing Steven new to riding would not be comfortable going any quicker. After some time riding Susan suggests they head back to the stables for the horses to be washed and some morning tea. "Race you back," she yells and without hesitating canters her horse, leaving Steven to slowly make his own way back. When Steven finally arrives, Susan is already off her horse and the horse is unsaddled and being brushed down. "Why did you leave me out there on my own?"

"I couldn't help it; cantering is my favorite gait and I just had to do it. You will love it too when you learn to rise to the trot." Without realizing it Susan had just invited Steven back.

"Be glad to learn," responds Steven with a grin from ear to ear. Together the two walk hand in hand back to the house, with Molly in tow. Steven's walk feels very awkward after just having his first ever horse ride.

Back at the house, Steven is offered a shower by Christopher. "How stupid of me Sir; I didn't bring a spare set of clothes."

"Yes; I was expecting as much, so I had the maid buy you a set." Steven rings the bell and the maid enters the foyer with the clothing. Embarrassed, Steven takes the clothes and follows the maid to the bathroom. Luckily

Susan is blind he thinks to himself, comes in handy at times. After showering, the maid gives Steven a picnic basket and Susan this time leads him to the tree in the field in the front of the property, to eat under the tree where they first met. Steven spreads the blanket and they both sit. Molly chases butterflies. Now is my chance thinks Susan. "Before we eat, if you don't mind I'd like to know who I'm eating with." She faces Steven as if she can see him, hands reaching out towards his face. "Is it okay if I feel your face?"

"Sure, no worries, help yourself." Steven sits up straight and holds his head very still. Susan places her hands on his face and starts to feel. She feels a high forehead with a razor cut short hair style. Running her fingers down his face she pictures how the features create the face in front of her. Hairy brows above pop out big eyes. "Have you got dark hair?"

"Yes, how do you know?"

"I can tell by your brows."

"Wow!"

Continuing down the bridge of his nose she can feel a straight but short bone with narrow nostrils. She spreads her hands across his cheeks and can feel stubble. "When was the last time you shaved?"

"This morning, early."

"Your hair must be black." Black shave mark, Susan loves this on a man.

"Yes that's right." Steven is truly amazed. Trailing her fingers down the jaw bones till her fingers meet in the middle of his chin she can tell he has a square jaw and chin with a dimple in the middle. Only one dimple on his left cheek though. Susan pictures a very handsome man in her mind. "Now I just need to know the color of your eyes."

"They are blue."

"Stand up, so I can feel how tall you are, please." Steven rises to his feet, followed by Susan. She reaches up and states "my guess is about six foot tall."

"Close enough." Without a pause, Susan runs her hands down to Steven's shoulders and over his chest and arms. He is a broad man and with great muscle tone. He obviously works out. Starting to feel romantically uncomfortable, by such a beautiful woman rubbing her hands on his body, Steven grabs Susan's hands and says "Let's eat." Disappointed this fun time is over, Susan sits back down. Together the two sit uncomfortably eating in silence. With the meal over, the two walk arm in arm back to the house. Seeing the smile on both faces, Christopher is most pleased.

Without actually stepping back inside, Christopher thanks Steven for coming, hands him his bag of clothes and bids him farewell. "Before I leave, Sir, may I please have the pleasure of taking Susan to dinner tomorrow night?" Christopher looks at Susan and sees her shy blush and coy smile. "I'll discuss it with Susan and call you."

"Okay Sir." Steven takes out his note pad and pen and hands Christopher his number, shakes hands, kisses Susan's hand and tells Michelle it was nice to meet her and heads down the stairs.

Once inside, Christopher interrogates his daughter on her date. He is happy with the result and wastes no time in ringing Steven to give the okay to take his daughter out for dinner. Meanwhile Michelle questions Susan on the looks of Steven. "So sis, his looks; explain them to me."

"He is so good looking. Black razor cut short hair, straight nose and strong jaw. He works out too. I picked him as about six foot tall."

"Well done sis, that's exactly how I would have described him too." Those descriptions are very similar to Lola's description of the arsonist. Surely not! Michelle decides to research him, just in case. With the date over, Michelle says her goodbyes and leaves; Susan blissfully goes to her room, anticipating her upcoming dinner.

Chapter Nine

The night arrives, Steven with excitement gets all dressed up in his best after five clothing. Looking at his image in the mirror; he is quite satisfied with the result. He eagerly drives to pick Susan up. On arrival Susan is already waiting on the front veranda. She is dressed in a red tea length, heart shaped bodice, fitted dress, accentuating her womanly curves. She is accessorized with black heels and a black clutch purse; beautiful. This is clearly a woman who knows how to appease a man's' eyes.

Christopher emerges from the house, holding a camera. "Now to catch a photo of the two of you," he states. Standing arm in arm the photo is taken. "Steven, I know you're wondering why I would take a photo of you both when Susan can't see; but you need wonder no more. You see I own 'Walker Electronics' and I had the guys in the workshop design me a camera for the blind. Not only does it print the image in 2D but it also connects to a special printer which can print in 3D, so Susan can feel the photo."

"That's amazing Sir. Are you going to start selling the cameras in your stores soon?"

"Once the trail with this test model is finished and I'm satisfied with the result. Susan will be my expert. Anyway expect lots of photos from now on. Oh and just so you know I took some of you horse riding yesterday." Oh just great, Steven thinks to himself. "Anyway enough talking, time to go to dinner. Have fun you two." With that, Steven escorts Susan to his car.

Steven takes Susan to Fairs Oak Avenue and pulls up in front of the most romantic restaurant he knows in all of Pasadena; 'The Raymond Restaurant'. Steven gets out throws his keys at the valet and opens Susan's door. "Inside or outside, which do you prefer?" Asks Steven"

"Outside, I love the outdoors." With that, the two take a table outside. "I love the Raymond hotel; I just love how the eatery is originally a workers cottage and how they have transformed it into this beautiful restaurant."

"So you've eaten here before?"

"Many times; but that's okay, it's one of my favorite places to eat." The waiter comes to take their order. Steven orders the finest bottle of wine and requests Long Island Roast Duckling with fresh Pomegranate and Cranberry sauce. Susan orders Soft Shelled Crabs Salad. "Well my father pretty much told me all there is to know about you, apart from your family," states Susan, trying to start conversation. This eating in silence the way her father likes to do is no fun at all. In fact Susan finds it boring. "Well, there isn't much to tell really. I have no family, it's just me."

"Oh, how sad."

"Yes my mum died giving birth to me and I've never known my father."

"Oh, I'm sorry to hear that." Maybe eating in silence is better after all. What to say next? "Actually we have something in common. My mother died while giving birth to me also. I was named after her. Explains why Daddy and Michelle are so protective of me."

"Really I wondered where your mother was but was never game enough to ask. I saw a photo in the sitting room of your father and a woman who looks just like you and a young girl. I thought it was of your parents and Michelle, is that right?"

"Yes that's right."

"You look just like your mother. The likeness is amazing." Susan gives a coy smile, secretly pleased as this is a huge compliment for her, because she thinks her mother was beautiful. The waiter arrives and asks about dessert. Susan doesn't want any; so Steven declines the offer as well. Steven pays the bill and asks the valet to get his car.

The drive back to Susan's is accompanied by pop music. Something; anything is better than silence. Once back at the mansion, Susan offers Steven inside for an after dinner drink. Together the two sit on the swing chair and gently rock back and forth. Susan expecting her father to interrupt them is surprised by his absence. "Excuse me Steven I'd like to speak to my father just for a moment."

"Of course." Steven's heart begins to pound in fear of what Susan needs to speak to her father about. A few minutes pass and Christopher walks to Steven with Susan. Looking very professional with a poker face, Christopher asks Steven; "It's Michelle's thirtieth birthday in a fortnight and I'm throwing her a party. Susan would love for you to attend, do you think you could make it?"

"When exactly is the party?"

"October 31 is her birthday so the party is on that same night and because of her birth date the theme is Halloween."

"Yes I'd be delighted to come. Thank you Sir."

"Make sure you come dressed in costume. Come at eight pm." Christopher says as he walks away.

"So what will you go dressed up as Susan?"

"I'm going as Cruella De Ville."

"I like it, who do you think I should go as?"

"Umm I don't know. I think I'll wait and feel to see if I can guess. I think that will be fun."

"Oh you do, do you?"

"Yeah feeling your face was heaps fun." That same coy smile takes over Susan's face. Love that smile, thinks Steven.

"I'll have to give it some thought."

Hand in hand they both sit on the swing for quite some time. Before long it's Midnight. "Well time I was heading home." Steven leans toward Susan and for the first time their lips meet. Gently but passionately they kiss. Susan has never known a kiss affect her the way this one just has. Am I falling in love already?

Meanwhile back in Los Angeles Michelle is on the computer; researching Steven Sheppard. Nothing comes up, not even a car registration. Strange; note to self: write down Steven's number plate.

Chapter Ten

The night of the party arrives. Susan is buzzing around with excitement. Michelle is not so happy. "Excited Sis?" Asks Susan

"Not really."

"Aw, why not?"

"Just not that excited about reaching the big 3-0. Not to mention everybody will now know my age and the reminder that my biological clock is ticking and I still don't have a boyfriend."

"Just why is that Sis? You're so beautiful"

"Maybe only beautiful on the outside; inside ugly. I'm too suspicious of everyone. Must be the Detective in me. Is it any wonder I went into that line of work?"

"You might be suspicious of people, doesn't mean you're a horrible person. I think you're beautiful in every way."

"Aw thanks Sis."

"Tell me, who are you dressed as?"

"Cinderella's evil step-mother."

"Good one. I wonder who Steven will come dressed as?"

"Well we're about to find out; here he comes now."

"Don't tell me; I want to feel and guess." As Steven takes a park and steps out of the car, Michelle can hardly believe her eyes. She can't believe he came dressed like this. She whispers to Susan "I don't think you will like it." And walks away, jotting down Stevens number plate. Why would he choose that particular character? Is he the killer?

"Good evening Cruella De Ville." You look beautiful. I especially like your spotted outfit.

"And good evening to you Sir. Come, let me touch to see who you are." Steven climbs the steps onto the veranda and walks over to Susan. Susan reaches out to touch him. She starts at the head, he is wearing a hood. Trailing her fingers down the hood, she can feel the hood attached to a loose dress. Maybe a super hero thinks Susan. Susan runs her hands down Steven's left arm onto his hand; no clue there. She runs her hand down his right arm. His arm is bent at the elbow, so she trails the arm to his hand. Susan can feel a pole in his hand. Moving her hands up the pole, she feels a scythe.

"You're the Grim Reaper!" Susan exclaims. Michelle was right; she doesn't like it.

"Yeah, wicked, hey?"

"Extremely!" Susan comes to the conclusion that Steven's definition of wicked and hers are completely opposite.

"Come through to the back, the party's started."

"Am I late?"

"No, Daddy told you eight so he can introduce you to everyone at once."

At the back door is Christopher dressed as Dracula. He announces to all guests that Susan's boyfriend has arrived and would like all to acquaint themselves with him. Steven looks around, everywhere is people in costume. There is The Incredible Hulk, Jason from 'Friday the Thirteenth', Witches, Aliens, The Devil, Evil Angels, The Mad Hatter, Red Riding Hood Wolf, Scarecrows and of course Michael Myers himself from the movie 'Halloween'. Steven whispers to Susan "Boyfriend?"

"That's Daddy all over. He likes to be in control of late I've noticed."

"No complaints here; I quite like his announcement." Steven takes Susan by the hand and enters the crowd. People come at them from all directions to introduce themselves. It's quite daunting for Steven.

Christopher announces let's get this party started and points to the DJ. Monster Mash, then Monster's Holiday and Thriller plays extremely loud. When Thriller plays the whole crowd gets up to do the dance, except Susan that is. Steven and Christopher suggest standing with Susan but she insists they join the crowd. Michelle can spot what her sister wants and pulls both Christopher and Steven in beside her. The dancers dance away, turning their back on Susan. Molly takes off around the front of the mansion, growling. Susan listens for her growls and follows her. At the front of the mansion Molly's growling intensifies and Susan calls "Come Molly, come girl." Molly stays put, growling more so. Susan hears in a scary voice "DIE." Terrified, Susan turns to run back around the back of the mansion. She doesn't get far when from behind she is jumped on, landing face first into the grass. She is then flipped onto her back with the villain straddled over her. Susan takes several punches to the face, then the villain starts to punch her in the body. Susan being knocked out at the first punch cannot scream. Molly goes berserk at the villain. She claws and bites the arms and legs of this vicious man, shaking her head while she bites deeper, still growling. She has a firm grip on his arm. The man rises to his feet and swings Molly into the mansion wall. Molly lets out a huge yelp, releasing the man at the same time. The man unable to hear music runs off. Molly limps over to Susan and lies by her side, whimpering and licking her master's wounds. At the back of the house the dance is over and no-one can see Susan. They seek her out, calling her name. They all run round the house spotting Susan lying flat on her back, unconscious and bruised. Steven and Michelle run to her aid. Christopher immediately dials 911. Susan is taken away in an Ambulance and Steven announces the party is over and for all to leave; except Steven, who is asked to accompany Michelle and himself to the Vet and then the hospital. Steven picks Molly up and puts her into Christopher's four wheel drive.

At the Vet molly is checked. Michelle asks for a scraping to be taken under her claws for DNA testing. X-rays are taken, Molly has four fractured ribs. She will need some time in the hospital but will survive. With that the three travel to the hospital. "Not again," Michelle breaks into sobbing. "Michelle; calm down, everything will be alright," states Christopher.

"You don't know that Daddy. You saw how messed up her face was."

"Well let's not jump to conclusions. Wait till we hear what the Doctor has to say." They arrive at the emergency department and are immediately allowed in to see Susan. She has regained consciousness and immediately asks the wellbeing of Molly. "Molly will be alright," Christopher answers. "Do the Doctors know anything about your condition yet?" he adds.

"I'm about to go to x-ray as I was not only hit in the face but also on my body." She opens her dress to reveal more bruising. Michelle asks "Do you remember hearing or smelling anything?"

"All I remember is Molly running away growling, so I went to get her and then I heard a man say in a deep

scary voice 'die' and I started to run away and that's all.
Next thing I know I'm in hospital. Sorry I ruined your
party Shell."

"You didn't ruin it. Whoever did this to you did, and if
I ever find out who it is I will kill him." She glances at
Steven, feeling shame and guilt for ever believing it may
have been him. Steven gives her a nod, secretly knowing
he was on the top of her suspect list. The nurse comes in
with a wheel chair to take Susan to x-ray.

On return from x-ray they all find out Susan has received
a hairline fracture on her left jaw and several broken
ribs. "She will have to spend a few days in hospital for
observation. I also want to do another brain scan just
to err on the side of caution. I don't believe anything
will be wrong, considering Susan is lucid. She will need
a liquid diet or soft foods only. Bring her back in six
weeks and we'll do another x-ray to check the jaw bone
has healed." A break to the left jaw means she was hit
hard with the right hand, possibly meaning the attacker
is right handed concludes Michelle; her inner detective
at work again. They stay with Susan for some time and
then all leave her to get as good a night sleep as she can.

Chapter Eleven

Michelle organizes a few days off work and decides to stay at her father's until Susan is out of hospital. She hopes she might get the chance to speak to her father and find out why he was at the Belief Church. Remembering how touchy he was about the issue of his library; which everyone in the house knows about, he just may be more so over something no-one knows about. It's late at night so Michelle decides to approach her father tomorrow about it.

The day is beautiful and after breakfast Christopher announces he is off to visit Susan. "Are you coming Michelle?"

"I will take my own car and check in on Molly on my way, I'm sure Susan will enquire about her."

"Good idea. Well I'm off, will meet you there."

"See you soon." Michelle heads back to her bathroom to brush her teeth. She can't stand brushing then eating. Christopher heads out the door. Coming down the stairwell Michelle passes the library, noticing that her father has left the door slightly ajar. That library, that darn library. Why is it so important to her father? She wonders. Maybe she can find that out too while she is here. Obviously her father was too concerned about Susan to ensure the library door was shut properly. She heads to the vet.

Molly is still sedated. The vet tells Michelle he would like to keep her there and sedated until Susan is home, so that Molly does not fret too much. "The scraping from under Molly's nails, are they ready to collect?" Enquires Michelle. The vet retrieves the scraping and Michelle leaves and stops by the police station. "Any news on who was at my fathers the night of the party," she asks Detective Oliver.

"Nothing as yet. We found a shoe print and took a mold of it. A size eleven men's Nike. A pretty common size and brand, suggests the man is approximately six foot tall. The sniffer dogs just kept going around in circles close to the bushes. Seems he appeared and disappeared into thin air."

"Do you think the bashing is connected to the car crash?"

"We can't say for sure, but it's a possibility."

"A possibility; I'd say for definite it's connected. Someone wants my sister dead but why?"

"We'll have to look into that."

"That would be helpful!" Michelle states sarcastically. She leaves rather annoyed, not bothering to tell them of the scrapings. She will get the analysis herself. They are hopeless, completely hopeless.

At the hospital Susan is looking bruised but happy. She is amazing how she can be so positive with all she has endured. Michelle stays for about an hour and announces she is going. Christopher decides to stay and lunch with his daughter; he will be home in the late afternoon. Good thinks Michelle, it will give her some investigative time.

Back at the mansion, Michelle sends the maid to the shops to collect groceries for her stay, giving her a made up list of what she especially wants and then gives her the rest of the day off, stating she will cook tonight. With the maid gone, Michelle gets to investigating. First she covers the surveillance camera outside the library with a dark jumper and getting a step ladder she removes the bulb and bangs it on her hand until it blows. She replaces the bulb and puts away her dark jumper. She enters the forbidden library. That young girl obeying all Daddy says conscience pops into her mind as she feels guilt at the first step inside the library. Better with the Detective mind, she thinks and takes another step inside. The library looks just like any other library, so just what is so important in here. She searches the books on the shelves. She goes to the B section, nothing on the Belief Church. She goes to the desk; no locks. That's odd Michelle thinks, but maybe not since no-one is allowed in here. Pulling out all the drawers she finds nothing but her father's notepad and pens. The notepad is empty. The other drawers are empty except for a pistol in the bottom drawer. Michelle takes it out and opens the revolver; it's loaded. A laptop sits upon the desk, Michelle lifts the lid. Of course a password is needed. Without knowing the password she closes the lid again. Nothing suspicious so she turns to leave with her head still in a tilted position. From the corner of her eye she spots a bright green U on the spine of a book on the bottom shelf. She goes over to take the book. The book won't leave the shelf but pulls out halfway. Michelle hears a click and under the mat is a trapdoor opened up with stairs leading down. Michelle walks over and locks the library door and goes down the stairs. At the bottom is a room with a chest of drawers. Inside the top drawer are papers with the letterhead BELIEF CHURCH written on them. He has dozens of them. They are newsletters from the church. He does have something to do with this church. If he likes the church so much why has he never taken them to the church? She closes the top drawer and opens the second. Just a key is in this drawer. Michelle looks around the room and finds a keyhole in a statue in the corner of the room. She tries the key and it fits. As she turns the key a door swings open to her left. She looks through the door to a tunnel made of brick. She glances at her watch the maid will be back shortly with the groceries. Michelle goes to the main library and gets the blu-Tack. She takes an imprint of the key and locks the door again, puts the original key back and leaves the secret room. Ensuring to push the U book back in the shelf and laying the mat straight, she leaves the library. She rings the maid and tells her to get a bulb for the surveillance camera before she comes home as she has noticed that one of the monitors isn't working. Michelle has the camera fixed and is cooking dinner by the time her father gets home.

Michelle tells her father she noticed one of the monitors was not working and she sent the maid to town to buy a new bulb and some groceries and then gave the maid the night off.

Michelle has cooked apricot chicken and potato bake for dinner, to be followed with jelly and ice cream for dessert. As usual the two eat in silence; then it's off to the sitting room for a drink and some conversation. "So Michelle what have you been up to this past week or so?"

"Well my partner and I had to go and reinvestigate the Lawyers house. We came across a young girl who saw a man running away from the fire. But on the way there Daddy, we passed the Belief Church and your car was parked out the front. What were you doing there?"

"You must be mistaken Michelle. It must have been a car that looked like mine. I've never even heard of a church by that name." LIAR, why is he lying?

"Oh sorry Daddy my mistake," Michelle goes along with her father not to cause any friction or suspicion. The two stay talking for a while and Michelle finally says she's off to bed. Why lie, what's he got to hide? Michelle has a lot of mystery to uncover.

The next day Michelle makes excuses to go to the shops and will meet her father at the hospital again. Michelle heads straight to a Locksmith to get a key cut from the blu-tack mold. Next she drives to her own station to get the scrapings from Molly's claws DNA tested. Finally she arrives at the hospital. "You've been a long time." says Christopher.

'Yes, well you know women and shops."

"Hmm!" Susan is faring well. Her brain scan reveals no further damage. What relief the family feel. Susan misses Steven but is comforted by the fact that he has plans for them both when her bruises fade. He has left a message with her father telling her to wear casual clothes. After an hour or so Michelle and Christopher both leave. They will be back tomorrow they reassure Susan.

The night is uneasy. Michelle can sense her father is on edge. Does he suspect she knows he is lying about the church or is it because he feels guilt about lying? Michelle decides to leave the evening free of such talk, instead focusing on Susan and Steven's next big date. "So where is Steven taking Susan on this date?"

"I honestly don't know, he just said it will be real casual this time."

"Susan sure sounds excited about the date anyway."

"Yes, I'm sure she is; he's a good man." Well of course Daddy would think that way, Michelle thinks to herself. She did after all hear Steven call her father Sir. Any man willing to do that is a good man in her dad's eyes. But maybe he is; after all Michelle had miss-judged him herself. Christopher heads to bed and Michelle stays up to watch some television.

In the morning, Christopher is at the breakfast table by himself. He realizes Michelle must be sleeping in after a late night and leaves for the hospital without her. Michelle didn't sleep in; she needed another excuse to be by herself today. She immediately heads to town after breakfast and goes straight to the Locksmith. He has made the key. She heads back to her fathers and upon entering the mansion, she remembers what Detective Oliver had to say about the man appearing and disappearing into thin air. She walks over to the shrub outside the veranda and moves the plant foliage around. Under the foliage she spots a trap door with a key hole. Michelle takes the key from her pocket and inserts the key into the hole. It fits; it's the exact same key as the one for the statue. She enters the underground dungeon. Before her is the same brick tunnel. She walks the tunnel with many alleyways off both sides. She heads straight not taking any turns. The tunnel brings her to a door. Undoing the latch and walking inside she walks inside the small room under her father's library. Right in front of her is the filing cabinet. She decides to turn and search the dungeon. She can't believe all these years they have had a hidden dungeon under the mansion and no-body knew except her father. As Michelle is about to take the first turn into the first alleyway her phone rings. It's the Sheriff from her department. The Belief Church Orphanage has burnt down, killing several people. She must leave immediately. She abandons the search of the dungeon and goes back inside to pack. She rings the hospital and speaks to her father and Susan to apologize and leaves for Los Angeles.

Chapter Twelve

Back at the station Michelle learns that luckily the children of the Orphanage were all away for the day on a field trip. The fire was deliberately lit and picked for today because the children were away. The Sheriff believes this fire is connected to the Lawyers house. Michelle and Donna are sent to the crime scene. They arrive at the Belief Church and are both shocked to see the main church still standing but only the Orphanage burnt to the ground. Obviously an accelerant was used to burn the building in such quick time and also in broad daylight. The two Detectives go inside to question the Minister of the church. The Minister is Brother Davis. After introductions, the Detectives get right to work. "Can you think of anyone who would want the Orphanage burnt down?"

"No."

"Maybe a child who grew up here?"

"No."

"Do you think the fire is connected to the Lawyers house not so long ago?"

"NO."

"You can't think of any reason why there may be a connection?"

"No."

"No, is that all you can say?"

"I'm a man of few words."

"And why is that, trying to hide something?"

"No, got nothing more to say is all."

"Hmm." It dawns on Michelle she sounds like her father. "Did you know a Peter and Shirley Bradford?"

"No, never heard of them."

"Never heard of them! It was headline news. That's the Lawyer's home that burnt down earlier this year."

"We don't buy the paper here or have television or radio. No media allowed."

"Ironic isn't it? Because now the Church is smothered with media." The Minister stands dumbfounded, having no answer to the statement. "So now Brother Davis, how does the Belief Church operate?"

"It's different to other churches. We don't hold services for the public; our service is within the Church itself."

"What do you mean?"

"All our members dedicate themselves to the Belief Church and work within the Church, helping the Children in their spare time."

"How does the church get the finances to do such work?"

"Our members are generous and give from their own pockets and the government fund us as well. We also have shops and own franchises' to which the proceeds come to us."

"Just how wealthy is the church?"

"Wealthy enough."

"Exactly how wealthy?"

"If you want that sort of information, you're going to need a search warrant."

"We'll be back then Brother Davis. I'll want to see finance reports for all this year and newsletters things like that. Communication within the Church."

"Finance reports yes, but we don't communicate with newsletters, it's all by word of mouth."

"Finance reports it is then. Good day." The Detectives leave.

"He's lying," states Donna

"Through his teeth," agrees Michelle, knowing all too well about the newsletters.

"They fundraise, own businesses and yet have never heard of Mr and Mrs Bradford's house being burnt down; as if?"

"Yeah let's go get that warrant."

Back at the church with the warrant Donna and Michelle are given the current and the last years finance books. They ask to be shown through what is left of the church. Brother Davis takes them for the tour. All that is left is the entrance, Minister Davis' office, bathrooms and the service room. The service room looks like any other church, with a cross above the pulpit and rows of pews. "That's it, that's all that's left?" Questions Donna.

"Until we rebuild the Orphanage."

"I wouldn't rush into that just yet. It's still a crime scene and can't be touched," states Donna.

"Not to mention that you probably won't get permission to rebuild the Orphanage," injects Michelle

"Why?" Asks Minister Davis

"Well if someone wants the orphanage burnt down, they just might do it again and we don't want to put young lives at risk, do we?"

"No of course not, but if you ever catch who did this, we could rebuild; right?"

"We'll have to investigate that." With the finance ledgers in hand, the Detectives leave. "We'll be back again for more if we need," Michelle adds as they walk out the door.

Back at the station, the detectives take a ledger each and start to go through them. Nothing of importance shows up. The ledgers are full of finance details mainly for the children, food clothing, energy bills; that sort of thing; also the donations and funds raised. Donna notes down the name of the businesses involved with the church and Michelle researches the Belief Church on the internet. Nothing not even one site. Strange! Donna finds nothing suspicious with the businesses either. Just local fish and chips, hardware, grocery stores and such. Nothing out of the ordinary. With the ledgers completed, no clues to be found Donna rests her case on Minister Davis knowing nothing. But not Michelle she knows there is more and will find out through her father's newsletters. Knowing this though must be kept top secret, she cannot implicate her father to the sheriff. She loves him too much and he might not know or have anything to do with any of the arson cases. She decides to spend more days at her fathers to reinvestigate the dungeon when able. Having this knowledge bothers Michelle so much it interrupts her sleep and makes her grumpy through the days. She rings her father to organize her next sleep over.

Chapter Thirteen

Michelle arrives at the mansion to Susan buzzing around with excitement once again. It is the day of her casual date with Steven. The two have been dating for about three months now and with Christmas just a week away, Susan is as excited as ever. Steven arrives and takes Susan by the arm almost immediately. He asks Christopher if he might join him and Susan for the date to take some memorable photos. Christopher obliges and gets dressed casually and grabs the camera. The three are off, leaving Michelle alone. Time to investigate.

Michelle heads to the shrub out front and unlocks the trapdoor. She walks as far as her father's secret room and enters. She takes the pile of newsletters and finds underneath a birth certificate for an Ugnè Lanka . . . . Why would Daddy have this man's birth certificate and who is he anyway? Daddy has never mentioned him in their life. She takes the birth certificate and a dozen newsletters'; which is a year's supply as they come out monthly and quickly goes into town to photocopy all and put them back. She grabs a bite to eat while in town.

Meanwhile Steven has taken Susan to the Petting Zoo. They have patted the farm animals and are now in the marine section. Susan puts her hand into the water pond and feels sea stars, sea cucumbers and other sea life. The sea cucumbers are her favorite as they are so soft. Christopher snaps many photos. They decide to eat with the wildlife in the middle of the lions dens. The lions cannot be patted but eat while the customers eat. Susan is thrilled with the roar of the lions. Next stop is the Australian petting section. Here they get to feed and pat the kangaroos and wallabies. Susan cuddles a koala and Christopher snaps a lovely photo. She likes the prickly feel of the echidna's spikes. Friendly magpies and kookaburras allow people to stoke their feathers on their backs only. They leave the Australian area and head to where Susan is most afraid the Reptile and Amphibian Park. Here she gets a photo of her and Steven both holding pythons. She pats a giant turtle and loves to hold a frog.

Back at the mansion Michelle has put back the papers and has her copies in her locked suitcase in the boot of her car. She is back at the entrance to the secret room. Turning back she heads to the exit but decides to check out the individual tunnels. She follows each one so far, none really leading to nowhere except empty rooms. One tunnel has a bathroom in its room at the end; immediately below the bottom floor bathroom of the mansion. She has just one tunnel to explore. She gets to the end and finds a mattress on the floor with bedding and a lantern. A pile of clothes lay next to the mattress. Does someone sleep here? She inspects the mattress and notices hair within the bedding. She takes the tweezers and a plastic zip-lock bag she is carrying with her in case she found some evidence. She decides she will get the hair DNA tested. Remembering Molly's claws, she realizes her scrapings must have a match by now. With time against her, Michelle leaves the dungeon and heads back to her room. She likes the new decor and is happy with the result. She is not long back in the room when her family return from their outing. She sits and listens to the excitement of Susan and cannot wait for the development of the photos. Christopher announces if Susan is happy with these photos; his cameras will be in his shops by early the following year. The four enjoy the evening meal together and Michelle retreats to her room to soak in a nice hot bath to relax. She has lots to think about. Christopher goes to his private library, leaving Susan and Steven alone. "Join me on the swing?" Asks Susan. Steven gets up and takes Susan by the hand. As he does so, Susan can feel a scar on his left arm. She wonders what it is from. Sitting on the swing Susan asks Steven about the scar. She wants to touch it. Steven allows her to feel the scar. Rubbing her hand on the scar, she can feel a U shape on the tender part of the wrist. "What's it from? It feels like the letter u."

"I don't know, I've had it all my life. Maybe it's a birthmark."

"Oh, it's a strong birthmark to be able to feel it."

"Yes, I hate it. Please don't mention it to anyone. Most people don't realize I have it unless they accidently touch it like you just did. I'm most embarrassed about it."

"Of course, I understand perfectly." Together the two embrace and sit for as long as the cool air allows them to. "Well I'd better be heading off now," states Steven.

"Before you go, will you be having Christmas Day with us?"

"I'd love to, with your father's permission."

"Daddy won't mind. I'll tell him in the morning, he doesn't like to be disturbed in his Library. What present will I buy you?"

"Nothing, don't worry about a gift."

"I will so worry. I'll think of something."

"Okay if you insist. I'll ring you tomorrow to see if you got your fathers okay for me to come."

"I'm sure it'll be fine, Daddy likes you." Susan leans into Steven for a goodnight kiss and Steven kisses her and leaves. Susan goes to bed, completely in love.

Morning arrives and Michelle says she has work at the station and has to leave immediately after breakfast. Christopher and Susan decide to go Christmas shopping. Susan has thought of the perfect gift for Steven; she has noticed he doesn't wear a watch. She concludes he must rely on his cell for the time. A watch will cover his scar he is sensitive over. She gets her father to choose a nice one for him and for her father and Michelle she buys gift certificates in their favorite shop.

At the station Michelle requests the results of the DNA from Molly's scraping and hands over the hair for testing. The results had no match on the police computer, so another dead end. Susan locks them in her drawer for evidence and safe keeping. She tells the forensic she wants the results of the hair today. She gets on her computer and looks up Ugnè. It's a name from Lithuania. More interestingly she discovers it means 'fire' and is actually a females name. She decides to visit Lola and Minister Davis again.

Michelle has taken a photo of Steven still suspicious of him and shows it to Lola. "Is this the man you saw running away from the fire?"

"I really don't know. It's a long time ago and I didn't get a good look at him."

"Look closely, are you sure?"

"Yes, completely sure." Another dead end. Without positive I.D. there is nothing more Michelle can do. She thanks Lola for her time and goes to see Minister Davis.

Minister Davis is not happy with Michelle speaking to him on her own and asks "Is it a day off for you Detective? You don't seem to have your partner with you."

"Yes that's right, just thought I'd investigate the fire some more."

"Well maybe you'd better come back when you're on duty. I'm not interested in speaking with you right now." He turns to walk away.

"Is that so? Do you know an Ugnè Lanka?" Minister Davis stops dead in his tracks and turns to face Michelle. "Just as I thought, you do, don't you?"

"I never said that. Who is this person?"

"I was hoping you could tell me."

"I never said I know him."

"And I never said it was a him. How would you know that unless you know him?" Strange! It's a girl's name, Michelle thinks to herself.

"Sounds like a males' name, that's all."

"How would you know? It's a Lithuanian name." She pauses "it could be either to us Americans." No answer. "I know you're lying so you can deal with me or through the police department. It's your choice."

"Okay I did know a man of that name about thirty or forty years ago. He was a member of our church back then. Haven't seen him since." A lead, Michelle finally has her lead.

"Your church is wealthy, billions of dollars wealthy."

"Yes that's right."

"All that money from your members and the businesses?"

"Yes and fund raising and government funding."

"If you didn't know of the Lawyer, how come when you own so many businesses? I also notice you have a computer and printer. Why one of each, if all communication is by word of mouth?"

"The computer is for record keeping. Members and children mainly."

"Does it have the internet connected?"

"Yes."

"And yet you didn't know of the Lawyers house burning down? Why are you lying? What is the connection?" Again no answer. "I want access to your computer."

"Sorry Detective, you're going to need a search warrant for that and how are you going to achieve that without involving the station?" No answer. "Anyway how did you hear of the name Ugnè?" No answer again. "Well when you can answer me that, I'll be willing to cooperate with you, until then this conversation is over. Goodbye!" With that Minister Davis turns and walks away. Michelle is left standing not knowing how to solve this matter. She heads back to the station for the DNA results of the hair. The hair is an exact match of the scrapings from under Molly's claws. Detective Oliver was right, Susan's attacker did appear and disappear into thin air, under the shrub that is. Enough Mystery for the day, Michelle spends the rest of her day off Christmas shopping.

Chapter Fourteen

Christmas day has arrived. A whole year since the car accident and still no leads on who set the car alight. This really frustrates Michelle; she decides she'd better pay Detective Oliver another visit. The family and Steven all gather around the beautifully decorated tree for the present opening. When Steven opens his watch, Susan offers to put it on for him. Steven extends his hand palm down and Susan feels for his U scar under his wrists. Covering the scar with her finger she puts the watch on. Steven is most happy with the gift. In return Steven gives Susan a beautiful pearl necklace. Susan loves it, as she feels the double strands around her neck. After the present opening and breakfast they all go to the living area and sing Christmas Carols. They decide to go swimming in the heated pool for most of the day. By afternoon Christopher is tired and decides to go for an afternoon nap. Susan asks Steven and Michelle will they go for a horse ride with her. Michelle declines and says it would be good for the two to have some alone time.

So they head for the stables, leaving Michelle alone with one thing on her mind, the dungeon.

Michelle heads into the dungeon. She can immediately hear noise in the first tunnel to her left, the one that had the bedding. She enters the room and spots a rat running away. On the bed is a man. Michelle says "who are you?" Immediately the man gets up and runs at Michelle and with impeccable force hits her in the jaw. Michelle is thrown backwards hitting the floor like a ton of bricks. The man jumps on Michelle and holding her by the shoulder lifts her head and drops it onto the concrete floor again and again. When Michelle is unconscious, he lifts Michelle and carries her outside and lays her on the ground in front of the steps. After placing her to look like she fell down the stairs, he rubs some of Michelle's blood on the stairs in several places and quickly grabs a bucket of water and cleans up the blood back in the dungeon. He puts the bucket back and goes back to his room in the dungeon.

Meanwhile out in the field Molly starts to whine and keeps turning back to the house and goes to Susan and barks. "I think Molly has had enough," states Susan

"I agree."

"Let's go back." The two ride back to the stables. At the stables Molly is not happy; she is still whining and sniffing the air. She runs back and forth barking at Susan. "I think Molly is trying to tell you something Susan."

"Maybe its best if we leave the horses tethered for now and see what's bothering her." As they round the front of the mansion, Steven lets go of Susan's hand and runs screaming Michelle as he does so. He reaches Michelle and immediately dials 911. Susan can hear what Steven is saying to the operator and tries hard to run to Michelle's aid. She reaches Michelle and Steven tells her "GO WAKE YOUR FATHER NOW."

"DADDY, DADDY, COME QUICKLY ITS MICHELLE!" Christopher jumps off his bed and races down the stairs. "What's wrong?"

"I'm not sure but I know Michelle is hurt." Christopher takes Susan by the hand and they both go out the front together. Christopher can see blood on the steps and sees Steven carrying out CPR on Michelle. He rushes to help. Together they manage to keep her alive until the Ambulance arrives. Michelle is rushed to the hospital. At the hospital Susan now realizes what her father and Michelle went through each time she was in here, the tears start flowing. Steven takes Susan in his arms and comforts her. The Doctor arrives and states that Michelle is now awake and stable and can have her family go in to see her. "What happened?" Christopher immediately wants to know.

"I have no idea."

"It looks like you fell down the front steps."

"I must have as I can't remember anything."

"What is the last thing you remember?" Asks Steven.

"I remember all day except for this. I remember you and Susan were going horse riding. I must have been going to join you and fell."

"Luckily Molly has great senses, she alerted us to what happened," says Susan.

"Yes good Molly. I'm lucky to be alive. Look guys I'm glad you're all here but I feel really tired. Do you mind if I go back to sleep?"

"Not at all, we'll come back later," announces Christopher. The family all give Michelle a kiss and leave the room. Out in the foyer Christopher asks the Doctor "Is it normal for Michelle to be this tired?"

"Yes perfectly normal after bumps to the head. She'll be sleepy for a few days. We'll keep her in for observation and until she can stay awake for most the day."

"What exactly is wrong with her?" Asks Christopher.

"She has concussion, but luckily no broken bones. Just had to stitch the cuts in her skull and jaw and wait for them to heal and that will be all."

"What about her memory, will she ever remember what happened and why?"

"Trauma does this often to a person. It's common not to remember." Christopher thinks of Susan who still cannot remember her accident. "Thank you Doctor." The three leave the hospital. Another Christmas wrecked. You know what they say; things happen in three's thinks Christopher. What will next Christmas bring? No; he shakes the idea out of his head.

Back at the mansion Steven cleans the blood off the steps for the family and decides he should leave. "Come again tomorrow," states Susan.

He kisses Susan goodbye, bids Christopher farewell and heads out the door. Christopher walks over to Susan, gives her a kiss on the forehead and goes to bed. Both are too upset to eat and therefore Susan also goes to bed.

Chapter Fifteen

Four days have passed and Michelle is allowed home. The nurse comes in and gives Michelle her only possession she had on her at admittance; a key from her pocket. Michelle cannot remember what the key is for. She puts it in her pocket again and forgets about it for the moment. Christopher and Susan arrive to pick her up, Christopher has organized with her Police Department for Michelle to have a few weeks off for recovery. He tells her she will stay with him and Susan. Michelle is happy for this as she misses her family while working. Christopher drives his two girls home, pleased to have his family with him.

Back at the mansion Michelle is given strict orders to take it easy and get plenty of rest. She decides to retreat to her bedroom. She pulls out the key and tries to remember what it is for. Nothing comes to mind. She decides it must have something to do with work and puts it in her briefcase to take to the station with her. Downstairs Christopher has given the maid the day off and he and Susan cook Michelle's favorite lunch; jacket potatoes filled with ham, capsicum, onion and cheese mash. After lunch the three just enjoy the afternoon talking. After a long day and a light dinner Michelle feels rather tired and heads to bed early. Christopher and Susan retire for the night as well. Due to Michelle's condition, Christopher has cancelled all New Year's Eve celebrations and thus the family have a quiet few days ahead.

Steven is back from flying and is visiting once again. Susan again wants him to go horse riding. So off they go. This time Christopher stays awake with Michelle to ensure she doesn't have any accidents. Steven has organized to take the whole family out for dinner. He takes them to a seafood restaurant. With everyone feeling satisfied he takes them back home. The four decide to have a game of Monopoly. Susan loves this as she hasn't played since before she was blind, in fact since she was a child. The best part of all is she only has to roll the dice and say 'buy'. She has trust that no-one will cheat. As a blind person she plays better, taking everyone's advice and wins the game. She feels quite pleased with her accomplishment. With the game over Steven decides it is time he heads home as the night is late. Christopher asks him back again on New Year's Day.

As Steven pulls up out the front it is raining. The day is spent inside. Michelle asks "Susan will you sing for us."

Susan feeling shy in front of Steven says "I'd rather not."

"Nonsense!" Christopher says in a stern voice "Come sing for us." Susan always obeying her father gets up to sing. Christopher sits at the piano and Michelle grabs her guitar as Susan wonders what to sing. "Well what will we play for you?" Asks Christopher. Susan walks to Michelle and whispers; she tells her father she will only need the guitar. Christopher takes a seat to watch with Steven, wondering what his daughter has chosen. Michelle starts to play and Susan sings 'No-one Needs to Know' by Shania Twain. Steven is gob-smacked. A smile overtakes his lips as Susan sings the song; really serenading him. Christopher has a shocked but pleased expression on his face. He cannot believe that shy Susan would be so bold. He is pleased. Boy, what a hint he thinks to himself. When the song is finished without even realizing it, Steven walks to Susan and gives her a passionate kiss. Christopher and Michelle stare in a state of shock, as Steven gets down on one knee and pulls a ring box from his pocket. "Susan, would you do me the honor of becoming my bride?"

"Yes" Susan shrieks with excitement "I love you Steven."

"And I love you." Steven puts the ring on Susan's finger and they embrace and kiss once more. Steven turns to Christopher and says "I ask for your permission to take your daughters hand in marriage."

"Permission granted." Declares Christopher. Christopher and Michelle clap and give the couple a congratulations hug. Steven whispers to Christopher "Sorry Sir, I did mean to ask you first but I became overwhelmed with the moment."

"That's okay my boy, I would have granted you permission to marry Susan. I trust you will take good care of her."

"I sure will."

Susan takes a moment to feel the ring. It feels beautiful. She asks Michelle to describe it to her. Steven takes out a piece of ring description paper from his pocket for Michelle to describe the ring. It is a three-quarter Old European Cut Solitaire in Cathedral Setting. It has half carat Baguette shoulder stones, four on each side on a twenty-four carat gold band. "It's absolutely beautiful Susan," whispers Michelle, taken in by the rings beauty.

"Tonight we celebrate!" announces Christopher. "We need to plan an engagement party," he adds. The maid is called in and asked to prepare for a celebration dinner. Luckily the maid had a roast Lamb meal planned. The dinner is actually eaten with talk as Christopher asks all about engagement party plans. January twelfth is the chosen date for the party. Michelle asks her sister can she take her shopping for her outfit. Of course Susan says yes. "You must have the wedding date picked by then to announce at the party," says Christopher."

"Umm okay," answers Susan. They wine, dine and dance the night away.

The next day Susan and Michelle hits the shops. Michelle helps Susan choose her engagement dress. It is a plum purple beaded one shoulder Chiffon Sheath, floor length with a split thigh high on the right leg.

Susan looks stunning in it. She also buys a clutch purse and heels to match. She finishes the accessories with silver and diamond drop earrings. They show the dress to Steven so he can buy a matching shirt.

The days leading up to the party are carefree with the family just chilling around the mansion.

Twelfth of January has arrived and Michelle helps Susan into her dress. She looks stunning. The night is perfect, not a cloud in the sky. A handful of guests arrive with their presents and are escorted to the back yard. Christopher has a marquee and seats all set up. Everyone takes a seat while Christopher invites Steven and Susan to the front to welcome all the guests. Camera flashes go off all around. Christopher asks the happy couple when the big day will be. They announce it won't be for eighteen months. The party gets under way. The night goes off without a hitch, which Christopher is most pleased about as he has secretly worried that something would go wrong once again. The guests and Steven leave and the family head to bed, leaving the cleaning to the hired help.

Chapter Sixteen

Michelle has fully recovered and is back in Los Angeles. She is at the police department and tries the key given to her in every lock. It doesn't open any. Confused Michelle puts the key back in her pocket and asks Donna where they are up to with the arson investigation. At least now she can get back on track. She reads through Lola's statement again, amazed at how the description given sounds like Steven. Next she reads the report from the visit with Minister Davis; nothing there except wealth. She looks through her drawers and finds a note with a number plate written on it. She researches the plate on the computer. The car belongs to a rental company. Great, what has that got to do with the investigation she thinks to herself and puts the number in her pocket. She has to remember why she had the number plate in her drawer. With no results for the day, she heads home frustrated.

At home she has a long relaxing soak in her spa bath. When she gets out she goes to her desk. In her locked drawer she has a heap of Belief Church Newsletters and a Birth Certificate for an Ugnè Lanka from Lithuania. She researches his name on her laptop. He disappeared thirty-four years earlier without a trace. He was a member of the Belief Church. She finds that the name Ugnè means 'fire' and is also a female's name. Strange that a man has a girl's name thinks Michelle again. Is this missing man involved with the fires? The computer alerts her to another fourteen missing persons in the same year; women by the name of Wendy Summers, Yvonne Smith and Natalie Bingle were never found. Wendy Summers disappeared nearly to the same day as Ugnè; is there a connection? She decides she will visit Minister Davis and talk to him about this Ugnè. As the Newsletters are in her desk at home she assumes she must have her own private investigation; she decides to visit Minister Davis on her own.

After a long unrewarding day Michelle heads to bed. She falls asleep quite quickly. Her night is disturbed with nightmares. She dreams of a man standing in thick fog coming towards her. As he gets closer with a look of anger on his face he looks remarkably like Steven. He punches her in the face. At that moment Michelle wakes up with a scream. Did Steven hit her? She must talk to Susan. She gets up and has a port to help her relax and get back to sleep. The next morning she feels drained.

Before heading to the station she visits Minister Davis. "Have you come with the search warrant?" Questions Minister Davis. What is he talking about?

"No, I don't have a warrant," states Michelle.

"Well then you can't have my computer. I didn't think you would involve the station." Obviously they have had private talks before.

"Tell me what you know of Ugnè Lanka," Michelle demands.

"I told you all I knew last time we spoke. He was a member of the Church but disappeared about thirty or forty years ago. I haven't heard from him since."

"That's all you can tell me about this man? Do you have any photos of him?"

"No photos and there is nothing to say about him."

"Well I've got to be heading to work; I'll be back when I need to." With the conversation over, Michelle heads to the department. The day at work is the same routine, nothing more develops. Michelle looks on the evidence board. They have nothing but photos of the crime scenes and the deceased. Nine people were burnt to death in the Orphanage fire. Michelle researches their names on the computer and all haven't any criminal offenses. She researches Peter Bradford and finds out that he became a wealthy and well known Lawyer about thirty-five years ago. That's the same time Ugnè disappeared; is there a connection between these two? She decides to visit the City Library to research the local Newspapers from thirty-four years ago. She will have to wait for a day off to do this. She struggles to continue the days' work after hardly any sleep. The next few days of work are the same for Michelle, no leads and no more fires. Thank goodness for that she thinks.

The nights have been hard on Michelle with her having the reoccurring dream every night, causing her to wake with a scream and sweaty; making her day time job so much harder. If only she could remember. She is convinced the dreams are the answer to her memory problems.

It's Michelle's days off and she enjoys a sleep in after yet another night of dreaming. She puts the number plate paper and key in her pocket and heads to the Library. She asks to be able to have a look on the computer at the City's Newspapers. The Librarian takes her to the newspaper archives computer and Michelle enters the year 1981 and types in missing persons. A list of names appears on the computer screen; among them are Ugnè Lanka and Wendy Summers. Ugnè disappeared on January seventh and Wendy disappeared on January fifth. Michelle researches bodies found. Eleven bodies in total were found that year. Two were men, both identified and of the nine women there are three Jane Does. Wendy Summers is not identified. Michelle prints out the pages of the newspapers for further investigation at home and heads to her fathers

At her father's house Susan is delighted to have her sister show up unexpected. She takes Michelle to a spare bedroom and shows her all the gifts they received from the engagement party; Michelle is impressed. Christopher is not at home at the moment, he had an appointment Susan tells Michelle. Michelle takes the opportunity to ask Susan about the night she fell down the stairs. "Let's have a picnic lunch together out in the field at the tree where you met Steven, so we'll know when Daddy is home," suggests Michelle. Susan agrees to the offer and the two head to the kitchen to pack the picnic basket. Michelle grabs the rug and they're off. Oh how the two sisters love this time together; it's been way too long since they have spent time just the two of them together. Michelle isn't sure Susan is going to love it by the end of the lunch; but it's a risk she must take.

Michelle spreads the blanket and they both sit. Molly sits next to Susan, Michelle gives Molly the dog treats and a bowl of water they packed for her. How to approach the subject of the fall and Steven is very difficult for Michelle. She decides to ease her way into it by discussing her injuries first. "So Susan, feel my head, I'm finally getting some hair back where they shaved me."

"You're not wearing the wig?"

"I was, but not here with you guys. No-one can see me. Anyway have a feel." Susan reaches her hand out and Michelle dips her head for Susan to feel. "Feels cool," remarks Susan. Michelle laughs at the remark. "So Susan, I've been having these nightmares since I've been home; I'm wondering can you tell me more about my fall to help me remember?"

"Well Daddy went to have an afternoon sleep and Steven and I asked you to come horse riding with us. You said it was better for us to have some time alone and decided to stay at the house."

"Then what happened?"

"With you I'm not sure but we were in the riding field and Molly kept whining and barking at me. I think she knew something was not right. I guess she could smell your blood." Susan gives Molly a loving rub on the head. "It was Steven who alerted me to Molly's actions."

"So Steven was with you the whole time?"

"Yes, except when he must have seen you laying on the ground. That's when he let go of my hand and ran to your aide. Because of Molly and Steven you are alive today and that only makes me love him more."

"Yes I understand."

"Why is it you ask of Steven's whereabouts?"

"These nightmares I have, I see a man surrounded by darkness as if in thunder clouds and he comes at me and punches me."

"I don't see the connection."

"I'm not saying there is a connection; but the man in my dream looks exactly like Steven."

"Are you sure of this? Do you think that your suspicions of Steven have you inventing a way to blame him for your accident?"

"No not at all, I just wanted to know more about how I was discovered. Are you sure I fell down the steps?"

"Just what are you implying? Of course you fell down the steps, they had blood on them which Steven was good enough to clean up so Daddy and I wouldn't get upset."

"I'm not implying that Steven did anything. I just wonder if my fall was an accident."

"I don't like where this conversation is heading; I suggest you leave. I won't tell Daddy you came and I'll make sure the maid doesn't as well."

"Oh come on Susan, don't take this personally."

"No! I'm serious, you can leave and give it some time before you come back so I can forgive you for your accusations." Michelle takes Susan by the hand to plead with her, Susan pulls her hand away, gets up and walks up to the house, Molly in tow. Michelle sits and cries; she was right, the picnic did not end well. She packs up the picnic and puts everything away and leaves.

Back in Los Angeles she again spots her father's car at the Belief Church. Is this the appointment he had thinks Michelle.

Chapter Seventeen

Christopher heads home and Michelle immediately goes in to see Minister Davis. "What has my father got to do with this church?"

"I really don't know what you're talking about."

"Don't lie to me, I just saw him here."

"Oh that, nothing for you to worry about."

"You tell me now!" Michelle demands forcibly, still in anger over the luncheon.

"Okay settle down; he only came with a donation to rebuild the orphanage." The Minister shows Michelle a check signed by Christopher. With this Michelle is satisfied and leaves quite proud of her father's generosity. Hold on Michelle thinks, I thought only members give financial help to this church she read in the evidence at the station. Is her father a member? She goes home confused. At home she opens her locked drawer to put away the key and the number plate note. She notices the pile of Newsletters from the belief church. It's a year's worth. She sits and reads them starting at the oldest. Nothing of importance in them, just the activities of the children, some drawings the children have done and the financial records, people who have donated and so forth. A name catches her sight, that name is Christopher Walker. Why has her father donated in the past year? Is he a member? Michelle decides when she can she will discuss this with her father; but due to the argument with Susan, it will have to wait some weeks. Michelle spends the rest of the day lounging around her apartment and after an early dinner heads to bed.

Michelle is in her father's Library; she notices a statue in the corner. In the statue is a key hole. Next minute she is outside and unlocking a trapdoor under a bush, she heads down the steps. Suddenly Steven is there surrounded by black, Michelle looks harder; he is in a room made of bricks. He runs at her and punches her in the face. Michelle wakes in a sweating frenzy, screaming. Steven did attack her. She remembers reading Lola's statement, a man fitting Steven's description was seen running away from the fire. She concludes Steven is the arsonist; she just has to prove it. After some time she falls back to sleep. She dreams once again, this time she is in the dungeon under her father's house, she opens a drawer and sees Belief Church Newsletters, many of them. She is in town at the locksmith and also photocopying the Newsletters. Again she jolts awake. Now she remembers everything. Her father is somehow involved with this church; she must continue with a private investigation. This; she is convinced will be a hard thing to do.

After an exhausting night, her father rings early. He wants Michelle to visit as Susan and Steven are out for the day. Michelle gets dressed and goes to her fathers. Her father has the maid cook a hot meal for lunch and together father and daughter eat in silence once again. After the meal Christopher asks would Michelle like to join him in the theatre room to watch a movie with him. She agrees, Christopher chooses a comedy and together they laugh at the movie. Michelle enjoys the moment; it's been years since they have watched a movie together. Christopher feels in the mood for some alcoholic drinks and asks Michelle to join him for a drink. They go to the sitting room. Christopher pours the drinks and they get involved in conversation of years past. Christopher has more and more to drink until his speech is slurred; Michelle has never seen her father so intoxicated before. She uses the opportunity to her advantage. "So Daddy, I saw your car at the Belief Church again." Christopher's eyes bulge at the statement. "This time Daddy, you cannot deny it; I went in and spoke to Minister Davis. He told me you gave him a donation towards the reconstruction of the Orphanage. That was kind of you Daddy, are you a member of the church?"

"No; I'm not a member," Christopher sobs as he says so. He breaks into a crying melt down. He becomes so upset that he is unable to speak in sentences. He just says over and over "Sorry, I'm so sorry." With how upset her father is Michelle leaves to get the maid. As she enters the foyer, Susan and Steven can hear the commotion.

Susan runs into the sitting room and hugs her father comforting him, telling him everything is okay. Steven helps Christopher up the stairs to his room. He takes his clothes off down to his boxers and puts him under the covers, Christopher immediately falls asleep and Steven leaves the room.

When Steven goes into the sitting room he hears Susan ask Michelle would she like to blame Steven for their father being upset, as she clearly blames him for everything else. An awkward moment for Michelle as she spots Steven at the doorway. Michelle stays silent. "WELL DO YOU BLAME STEVEN OR NOT?" Susan is yelling by this point. Steven coughs and interjects with "Susan, what are you talking about?"

"Michelle wants to blame you for the fires and I'm asking her would she also like to blame you for Daddy being upset tonight." Steven looks at Michelle with eyebrows raised. Michelle immediately turns a crimson red with embarrassment. She knew her sister was angry with her but not this angry as to blurt this out. "Tell him Michelle, tell him how you wonder if he is the reason you fell down the steps and how you are suspicious of all the fires and how you think Steven started them," Susan demands of Michelle. Michelle drops her head and admits to her thinking. "I haven't fully got my memory back but I am suspicious. I don't believe my falling down the steps was an accident."

"You do remember I was with Susan horse riding, right?"

"Yes," responds Michelle.

"Well how can you possibly think I have anything to do with your fall?"

"Well you got to me first and you were with a blind girl."

"HOW DARE YOU!" blurts Susan crying at the comment. She has never had her feelings hurt by Michelle like this. Steven puts his arm around Susan's waist. "What about Molly alerting us to the accident, explain that Detective," Susan adds with a trace of sarcasm.

"I'm sorry to upset you Susan; I just have to be certain. As for Molly I cannot explain."

"That's because there is nothing to explain," sobs Susan. "How can you hurt my feelings like this? You're not only attacking my fiancé but me also."

"So you think I was involved in the fires. Fair enough you didn't know me when the Lawyers home burnt, but I was with Susan in the hospital when the orphanage burnt down. How could I possibly be to blame?"

"Like I said I don't have all my memory back as yet. I forgot the burning of the orphanage took place at the same time as Susan was in hospital. Please forgive me Steven, I feel so bad I ever thought it could be you."

"Apology accepted; you took a bad bump to your head with the fall down the steps, maybe you need some more time off work. You're starting to grasp at straws." Susan cannot believe that Steven is just willing to so easily accept Michelle's apology. He might be but she is not. "Good night Steven, I'll see you tomorrow I'm going to bed," Susan says as she leans in for a kiss. "Night Darling, see you tomorrow."

"Good night Michelle," Susan adds grumpily as she walks past Michelle.

"Good night Susan; I truly am sorry."

"Humph!" responds Susan and walks out the room. Once Susan is out of sight, Steven walks to Michelle and states "The forgiveness is for Susan's benefit only, never make the mistake of blaming me again or else." Michelle feels really scared; or else what? Steven leaves without a good-bye and Michelle remains suspicious, especially with his last remark.

Chapter Eighteen

The next morning the air can be cut with a butter knife the air is so thick. Everyone feels uneasy. Christopher cannot remember how the night played out but can sense the uneasiness in the room. He demands to know what happened. Susan and Michelle are reluctant to say but due to their constant obedience they answer their father. Susan states "Michelle somehow thinks Steven is involved with her fall down the steps." Christopher is in shock. "Nonsense, how can you even think such a thing? He was with Susan the whole time."

"I don't know what got into my head Daddy but I feel ashamed. I keep having dreams of Steven coming towards me and punching me to the ground. It made me suspicious of him."

"That's just your head messing with you; you're trying too hard to join the pieces together, just let time take its course and the answers will reveal themselves."

"That's not always true Daddy; we have plenty of unsolved cases at the department."

"Yes but they are crimes; this is an accident and accidents happen."

"Yes but sometimes on purpose."

"There you go again, being overly suspicious. Put it out of your mind. How about you Susan? Are you okay?"

"I'm okay but I'm hurt by Michelle's accusations and wish not to see her for some time. I need time to calm down; she even made a comment about me being blind."

"Michelle how could you?" Christopher asks in an angry tone. Michelle breaks into a cry and responds with "I honestly don't know; I guess my anger took over when Susan told Steven of my suspicions."

"So Steven also knows; this is not good. Michelle I think it's best if you go home and I'll work on things here and contact you when things have settled." With that Michelle gathers her belongings and leaves in tears. Back at her house she is too upset to do any more investigating and mopes about instead.

The next day when Steven arrives he has plans to take Susan to the park; but Christopher has other plans. He tells Steven he knows about last night and needs to talk with him and Susan. Susan is not only upset by Michelle's accusations but is crushed by the blind comment. "Susan love, you need to understand that in the heat of the moment people can say or do things they don't mean to. Either that or they don't intend for the hurt it causes once the words have been spoken. They can never take them back, the most they can do is apologize for them and so long as they are sincere which I believe Michelle is, it's up to the hurt one to forgive. That's the only way this can be mended. Are you willing to forgive?"

"I don't know Daddy; I'm just so hurt by her words."

"Yes I can understand that; but that's because Michelle has been such a good sister to you. You two have never had an argument before. Michelle has always been like a mother to you, not a sister. She loves you very much." Susan sobs. "Come on Darling, Michelle is hurting as much as you," Christopher says as he gives Susan a cuddle.

"Just give me a month or so to myself and then I'll see her again. By then I will have enough time to think this through clearly."

"Okay a month it is. Now, don't you and Steven have a date? Off you go." Susan and Steven gather the picnic basket and head out the door.

While they are at the park, Christopher decides to watch the tape recording from the surveillance camera as he cannot remember much. He is shocked with his behavior but glad he didn't reveal any more information. Michelle and her suspicious mind he thinks. He keeps watching and listens to the argument. He is angered by the threat Steven makes to Michelle; no wonder she is suspicious of him. He realizes Michelle did not inform him of the threat. He concludes that she mustn't want Susan to know. He decides he will keep it that way but will let Steven know what he heard. Threatening his daughter will not be tolerated. He is so angered he leaves for the day with no destination in mind; he just does not want to be there when Steven gets back. He needs to pick the best time to say something and while he is this angry is not the time.

Christopher pulls up outside the L.A. Police Department and asks to see Michelle. Although he is too angered to see Steven, he will speak to Michelle about the issue. "Hello Daddy, I didn't expect to see you here."

"Hello love; yes I know, can we lunch together?"

"Yes of course, I'll just let Donna know." They leave together in Christopher's car. They buy fish and chips and eat together at the park. Michelle feels the tenseness between them and starts the conversation with "I truly am sorry Daddy."

"Yes I know that Darling. What I don't know is why you didn't tell me about Steven's threat he made to you."

"How do you know about the threat?"

"I watched the video footage." Oh, of course the cameras, thinks Michelle. "Why didn't you inform me of his threat?"

"I didn't want Susan to know."

"Ever the protective sister; Susan is lucky to have you for her sister, you know that don't you?"

"I'm sure Susan doesn't think so now."

"Oh she knows. We've had a talk this morning and she needs about a month and she'll be okay again. Just give her that space."

"Daddy, you're not going to say anything to Steven about the threat, are you?"

"You're damn right I am. No-one threatens one of my girls like that and gets away with it."

"Daddy, I wish you wouldn't, just leave it with me."

"I will not! I'm not a genie so therefore you do not get your wish this time. I will handle this matter."

"Hmm," Michelle sighs, leaving the subject alone. She decides to broach the other subject of the night. "So why were you so upset last night Daddy?"

"It saddens me to think those kids were so close to death, that's all."

"Is that all there is to it Daddy?"

"Yes and I don't appreciate your snooping around asking questions being suspicious of your own father. I gave the church some money to help refinance the Orphanage and that's all; so no more questions from you, do you understand?" Feeling intimidated Michelle responds with "Yes Daddy, I understand perfectly." The rest of the lunch is in silence. Christopher drops Michelle off and drives home.

He isn't home long when Susan and Steven return. Susan wants to soak in a hot tub and says good bye to Steven. She goes up the stairs. Steven watches her disappear and turns to say goodbye to Christopher. Christopher quietly walks over takes Steven hand to shake and doesn't let go. Squeezing Steven's hand tightly he whispers "Don't ever threaten one of my daughters again or you'll see my 'or else', understand?"

Steven gulps "Yes Sir."

"Good bye."

Steven leaves feeling shaken up that Christopher knows about the threat.

Chapter Nineteen

Susan and Christopher spend the days talking out Susan's emotions, Christopher trying to get Susan to understand Michelle's standpoint. He reminds her several times about Michelle's head injury and how it just might affect her thinking. Susan reveals to her father about Michelle's nightmares and how she sees Steven running at her and punching her. This makes Christopher all the more supportive of Michelle and her suspicions about Steven. He finally gets Susan to understand and Susan is more forgiving.

Steven has not shown his face since the argument, Susan wonders if he is upset with the situation and not forgiving after all. She not realizing her fathers' last contact with Steven asks her father will he give him a call and invite him over. Hesitant to do so, Christopher does as his daughter wishes. He picks up the phone and invites him to visit. Within an hour he arrives.

Walking up the steps looking sheepish, Christopher extends his hand and welcomes Steven back. Christopher invites them both to join him for a cup of coffee. Like the meal the coffee is drunk in silence. Once the coffee session is over Susan asks Steven would he like to have some fun horse riding. Before Steven can answer, Christopher intervenes with "Lets the three of us play a round of golf instead."

"Daddy I know you love the sport but I really cannot play when I'm blind."

"Nonsense! Don't let your eye sight ruin a good game. If you can ride blind you can play golf blind." Susan surrenders and accepts the challenge. Christopher drives them to the golf course and pays for the three to play. At hole one Christopher puts the ball on the tee for Susan and points her in the direction to swing; she cannot strike the ball. She once loved golf but now hates it; Steven, ever the gentleman goes to assist her. He stands behind her and with his arms around her and hands over hers he helps her swing the club. Susan has changed her mind; blind golf isn't so bad after all. For the whole eighteen holes Steven helps Susan swing the club. Susan has fun and lots of it at that. She wants to play again another day, Christopher watching the performance is not so keen. After golf they all go to the club and enjoy a meal together and then Christopher drives them home. Steven asks "Sir with your permission may I take Susan out tomorrow night?"

"Umm I suppose that will be okay. You are after all her fiancé." Steven is pleased with the answer; they can be a couple again.

"Wear jeans," he tells Susan. He gives her a kiss, bids Christopher farewell and is off.

Steven arrives after dinner to collect Susan. He takes her to the local Ten Pin Bowling Centre. The gutter rails are put up and the game begins. Susan's first ball gets thrown into the next lane. Steven helps out again. He stands Susan at the line, hands her the ball and tells her to keep her arm straight. She does as explained and succeeds, the balls rolls down her lane and knocks down some pins. Depending on the split of the remaining pins, Steven tells her where to stand. Susan finishes a good game, scoring 193; coming in second with Steven scoring 206. "You're quite the player," says Steven.

"I'm not too bad, we came often enough as children."

Steven walks Susan out to the car and opens the door for her. She gets in and when Steven turns to go to his own door, a man punches him, knocking him into the car door. Steven takes a blow to his stomach knocking the wind out of him. The man punches Steven again and again. Steven gets kneed several times in the stomach and groin area. Steven throws some punches but with the wind knocked out of him and the pain in the groin area his punches are not much use. Meanwhile in the car Susan can hear the commotion going on and locks the door. She is terrified, knowing there is a fight going on just outside her window. Again and again she can hear grunting and feel the car getting rocked as men are knocked against the car. Steven manages to connect a punch, knocking the man to the ground. He gets on him and punches him several times. The man kicks Steven off him and this time is on Steven. Steven managers to block several hits and instead of a punch gives the man a good scratch on the face. A family walk out to the car park and the man gets off Steven and runs away. The father of the family runs to Steven's aide. He helps Steven to his feet and offers to call 911. Steven says he is okay and with a bloody nose and lip and a black eye drives Susan home. Susan is distraught, crying the whole way home that her beloved Steven has also been beat up. The family man has given his phone number to Steven for a witness if needed.

Back at the mansion Christopher immediately rings Michelle to come with her investigative kit. Michelle arrives and asks Steven for a description of the man. Steven cannot really give her one as he didn't get a good look at him. The man was wearing a hooded jumper. All Steven can say is he was about the same height as himself and was really strong. Michelle takes a scraping from under Steven's fingernails for DNA testing. Christopher offers Steven to stay at the mansion for the night for safety. Steven thanks Christopher but declines the offer as he hasn't any clothes and goes home. Michelle stays the night since it is quite late. She again apologizes to Susan and says "With the evidence before me I am so sorry to ever have thought Steven had anything to do with my fall or the fires. I have to swallow my pride; please forgive me." Susan isn't happy it had to come to the conclusion of her fiancé getting bashed for Michelle to believe he is innocent but forgives her. She walks over to Michelle and gives her a cuddle "Of course I forgive you; I love you."

"And I love you. Thank you Susan; I won't be suspicious of Steven again."

The next morning Michelle goes to the Ten Pin Bowling Centre and searches the car park for any evidence; just some blood on the ground. She asks at the counter to see any video footage. The tape is produced; she watches it and says she will take the tape as evidence. She goes back to the spot where the fight took place and takes some samples of the blood with her. With nothing more to see she heads back to the mansion first to inform her father and sister and then drives to her station to have the evidence analyzed. The video footage she keeps to watch at home herself. The rest of the day is uneventful, thank goodness for that Michelle thinks. She checks on the results of the blood samples. The blood is an exact match for the hair and the skin scrapings from under Molly's claws. Whoever did this bashing of Steven is the same man who attacked herself and Susan. Why would someone want to hurt them? Is anyone safe? What about her father; he hasn't been touched? Surely someone wouldn't want to hurt her father; but they did hurt the beautiful Susan. Is this man responsible for Susan's car accident? These are answers Michelle wants. She will stop at nothing to get them. She has to wait a little longer for the results of the skin scrapings from under Steven's fingernails.

That night at home Michelle takes another look at the video footage. She pauses on places of interests and rewinds and re-watches if she spots something of interest. She pauses the tape on the back of Stevens' car as the number plate catches her eye. She opens her drawer and takes the piece of paper with the number plate written on it. It's the same plate. Why is Steven using a rental car? She decides she will check this out tomorrow. With her mind full of confusion and questions she goes for a long soak in the tub and heads to bed.

Michelle wakes up unusually early and realizes she didn't eat last night. She cooks herself a hot breakfast so she can concentrate well today. On her way to work she stops at the car rental company, showing her Detective badge she asks the name of the person the car Steven drives is rented to and how long he has been renting it. The counter girl gives the information. The car is rented to a Mr. Joseph Bradford and has been for nearly two years. Michelle writes the name down and thanks the girl. What is Steven doing with a car rented to Joseph Bradford? That name sounds familiar to her. Although she told her sister she wouldn't be suspicious of Steven again; she is.

Chapter Twenty

Steven stays away while his face heals. He finally after two weeks goes to see Susan again. She is delighted he has visited. She has been sitting and feeling her 3D photos of their time together. She has decided to put together a scrap book of all their dating life to tell their love story. She wants to actually pick a wedding date. Steven checks the calendar app on his phone to look at the next year's dates in June. "June seems such a long way away" Susan states. "We did tell our engagement guests it would be in eighteen months" Steven reminds Susan "Besides it will give us plenty of time to organize the wedding." Susan nods her head in response. "June fourteen sounds like a good date to me; right in the middle of the month. What do you think?"

"Yes I like that date too. June fourteen it is. Now where to get married is next on the agenda."

"Would you like a church wedding, in a park, or at the beach? The choice is yours," Steven leaves the options to Susan.

"I'd like to get married right where we met. At the tree in the front field; then we could have the reception here at the mansion."

"Well if that is what you want then that is what you can have." Susan is so happy. Together they continue to make the scrapbook.

Meanwhile in Los Angeles, Michelle is doing some research. She looks up the name Joseph Bradford. He is the son of the Lawyer whose house burnt down. Joseph was not a suspect but has not been seen or heard of since the fire. Has Steven got something to do with his disappearance, he is after all driving the car rented out to Joseph. Just what has Steven got to hide? Michelle knows she cannot approach Steven about this but must secretly investigate for the answer. She just has to discover a way of doing so. She checks on the skin scrapings from under Steven's fingernails; again they match the /DNA already collected. That's strange thinks Michelle; she must have scraped up the other man's blood and none of Stevens. She was hoping for a sample of both. She decides she will have to get a sample of Steven's DNA; even if it's hair. She drives to see her father and sister.

At the mansion Susan and Steven are now out in the pool. Michelle decides to speak to her father first. "So Daddy; did you decide not to say anything to Steven?"

"Oh, I said it alright!"

"So why is he here?"

"Susan could sense something was not quite right and she asked me to invite him over and I gave in."

"I see; say Daddy do you remember where you drove him home that night?"

"Yes I do; why's that?"

"Can you drive me there; I'd like to see what house he might have Susan move into once he marries her. Just want to make sure it's safe you know."

"Hmm good idea; I'll get my keys." Michelle goes out the back to tell Susan and Steven she is going out with their father and they won't be long. She asks the maid to keep an eye on them both. She gets into the passenger side of her father's car. Looking at the house, they both decide they don't like it. "It would be better if Steven does buy out of town. He was looking the day he broke down," states Christopher.

"I wonder what stopped him? He's had heaps of time to buy," adds Michelle.

"Hmm I wonder?" Christopher agrees. They are satisfied with the look and goes back home. Susan and Steven are back inside by now. Michelle says she has to leave and says her good-byes and is gone. "Where did you go Daddy," asks Susan

"Oh; nowhere important, just for a drive." Christopher decides to address the house shopping with Steven and if he is not serious about buying another place he might just buy them one for a wedding gift.

Michelle goes back to the station and finds out that Donna had organized for a search warrant on the Belief Church and can now collect the computer. The Sheriff tells Michelle she is the one who will research what is on the computer. He tells her to take it home and do so. Michelle is thrilled; she has her hands on that computer and she can do her own private investigation on it as well. "It has a strange password; it's Ugnè," the Sheriff tells Michelle "That's spelt U-G-N-E; the U is in capital and the E has one of those French marks over it." Donna and a colleague had already got the computer while she was at her fathers. Donna gets one of the junior officers to help her take the computer to her car. Michelle heads home to investigate the computer. The computer has nothing of interest on it; more or less the same stuff recorded in the Ledgers. Michelle tries to open an unnamed folder; it is blocked by another pass word. Michelle types in Ugnè; no luck, she needs the correct password. She decides it will need another visit to Minister Davis. She gets in her car and drives to see him. It is raining and she doesn't get far when her car loses control and she crashes into an electric light pole. The Ambulance rush her to the nearest hospital; where the family is contacted.

At the hospital the family are concerned for Michelle's welfare. She has suffered a broken left foot and a broken right forearm; not to mention her many bruises. The Doctor has said she will be in hospital for a week and will need three months off work for her injuries to heal properly. Christopher insists she stay at his home while she is healing. After several hours at the hospital, the family leave, with a promise to visit every day. As promised every day; Christopher and Susan visit Michelle.

The day has arrived for Michelle to be able to go home. Christopher and Susan are there to get her. They are both excited; considering the circumstances to have Michelle with them for three months. The accident has been a reality check for Susan and she is thrilled to have the opportunity to repair their damaged relationship. Back at the mansion, Christopher has organized for a carpenter to make half the front steps into a temporary ramp for Michelle in the wheelchair. He has also organized a room downstairs for her so she can stay on one level. Michelle hates not being able to walk or be independent; she will even need help with toileting and showering. She is not in a good mood. Christopher and Susan can sense this and leaves her alone for the afternoon. Michelle asks to be wheeled out onto the veranda to enjoy the sunshine. Christopher gives her a maid bell and asks Michelle "Would she like him to hire a nurse while she heals?"

Michelle says "No; she'd rather have Susan help her." Christopher is concerned about Susan being blind. "Oh Daddy, she may not be able to see but she hasn't lost her strength."

Christopher respects Michelle's decision and Susan is delighted that Michelle would prefer her help. The next three months are going to be awkward for the family but hopefully also successful.

A week has passed and Michelle and Susan have regained their closeness. It's Michelle's first visit back to the fracture clinic. The bones are healing well. The Doctor is happy that she is following orders and not using her arm or foot to weight bear. How could she possibly? Her father would have a fit. After good results, Michelle wants to go to the station and check in on things. At the station she finds out that the accident was caused by a mixture of a wet road and an oil spill. She is told it could have happened to anyone. Yes it could have but it didn't; it happened to me, thinks Michelle. In fact lots of things are happening to her family; but why? Michelle is once again suspicious, she will investigate this further.

Chapter Twenty-One

Steven has turned up to see Susan and hopefully take her out. Susan tells him that for the next few months all their dates will be at her house as she cannot and will not leave Michelle unaided. Steven although unpleased with the command, he is also understanding and hence gives into Susan. It's going to be a long ten weeks Steven thinks to himself; with Michelle constantly with him and Susan. Michelle is pleased Steven is unhappy with the way things are; she's not sure she likes this man. The next ten weeks will give her time to examine him closer.

Wherever Steven and Susan are on the estate, Susan insists Michelle is with them in case she requires her help. Horse riding is definitely out of the question. Susan gets Steven to push Michelle everywhere they go. They can go swimming, on estate picnics, sit in the veranda swing or lounge around the house but they must have Michelle with them. Susan is happy but Steven does not like it; as he feels he cannot be as relaxed with the suspicious Michelle around. He feels her eyes on him at all times watching his every move; sometimes he looks directly at her to call her bluff; but she just keeps on watching. He eventually turns away; admitting defeat. Every day Steven visits he gets a bit more agitated. If he had his way he'd stay away for a few weeks but Susan insists he come each time he is home. Michelle deliberately says "Does it bother you Steven that I am with you and Susan each time you visit?"

"No not at all, don't be silly," replies Steven, giving Michelle the most false sincere look she has ever seen.

"Michelle, Steven doesn't mind at all," intervenes Susan; not having a clue about the facial expressions.

"Oh goody; I'm having a ball joining in with you guys," Michelle cannot help but say. She gives Steven a sly smile. He responds with sticking his tongue out at her; somehow Michelle knows all too well that he isn't playfully doing that but means it rudely. "What will us three do today?" adds Michelle.

"How about some sunshine?" says Susan, she adds "A stroll around the fields?"

"Sounds great to me, that is if Steven doesn't mind pushing me," Michelle answers. She gives Steven another sly smile.

"Oh he won't mind at all, will you Darling?" Susan inquires of Steven.

"Be delighted to," he answers; right back to L.A. he thinks to himself. He is glad he met Susan and not Michelle that first day. How sisters can be so different, he wonders.

With the day's activity sorted they start their walk around the estate. Michelle's wheelchair carries the water bottle and the food. "It's amazing the different view and aspect you get of the estate when you don't have to worry about where you are stepping and can just take the time to look." Michelle says

"Yes I can imagine," says Susan "I have a complete different view of the estate since being blind, all on memory, but it's still beautiful."

"Sure is a nice piece of land your father has here," adds Steven. Is that his motive for wanting to marry Susan, for the property and money, wonders Michelle? She quickly shakes the idea out of her head; it makes it sound like Susan is incapable of being loved. She feels guilty for the thought. "You're right Steven, it is a beautiful estate, and we are blessed to have it. I know many people have nowhere to call home; it's all quite sad really," says Michelle. The afternoon sunshine disappears and dark clouds loom above, time to head back inside. As they near the steps, Molly runs to the bush and sniffs at the ground growling and whining. Steven is quick to call her back. "I wonder what has her so intrigued at the bush?" Michelle makes an inquisitive statement; already knowing the answer.

"It must be a field mouse or the like," answers Steven.

"Yes it must be," responds Michelle and then she concentrates on getting safely up the ramp with the hope of any suspicious thoughts not being revealed. Once inside the rain begins to fall, lightly at first but quickly turning heavy in no time at all; then as quickly as it started it finished. "Please Shell, tell me where the rainbow is," requests Susan "take a photo for me," she adds. "The rainbow is out the back over the stables; it's beautiful," Michelle answers as Steven wheels her onto the back veranda to get the photo. "These are memories I want forever; I miss seeing the beautiful rainbow God put in the sky," Susan says with a teary voice. Michelle sheds a silent tear herself. It dawns on Michelle just how her sister's life must be without sight; all she has are her memories. She also thinks about the things Susan will never see; herself in her wedding dress any future children; memories she will only hold in her heart, never in her mind. Michelle suddenly feels sad and asks to be taken to her room. Once behind closed doors she breaks into a weeping cry; a cry she has never experienced for Susan before. She feels extremely guilty of being suspicious of Steven but she realizes she must protect her every way she can. Letting go of her beloved Susan is very difficult. After some time alone she rings the bell to rejoin the others; Steven goes and gets her, unaware of what Michelle has just endured.

With night approaching, Michelle requests they order pizza for dinner and relax in the lounge to eat; Christopher gives his permission and the pizzas are ordered. Christopher gives the maid the night off; she leaves to visit family. With dinner over Steven stays a couple of hours more and then says he must go home as he flies tomorrow. Susan helps Michelle bathe and get into bed and then heads upstairs to her own room. Everyone falls asleep. Michelle is suddenly woken by noise in the kitchen. She can hear cupboard doors and the fridge being opened and closed. She knows someone is in the house; but also knows there is nothing she can do. Yelling won't help, as her father will never hear her and she doesn't want to risk Susan walking into danger. She lays silent and listens for the footsteps as they disappear into her father's Library. She remembers the bedding in the dungeon and wonders if someone is living beneath them. How often is that someone in the house at night, helping themselves to the pantry? She decides she must listen again tomorrow night and every night she is there. She actually feels quite scared at the thought.

The next night again Michelle is woken to noise in the kitchen and footsteps disappearing into her father's Library. She cannot wait until she is well again so she can investigate this properly. She decides not to warn her father or Susan as all the stranger does is go to the kitchen and back to the dungeon. She finds it strange how Molly with super strong senses doesn't seem to bark, growl or investigate what's happening. She concludes that it must be because Susan sleeps with the door of her bedroom closed.

The days pass and soon another week has also passed. Michelle is healing well and is starting to be able to use her arm again. She still cannot weight bear and is thus still confined to the wheel chair. Steven is visiting again; Michelle wonders if she should ask him to sleep a night to help with the intruder, but decides she had better wait until she is well enough to help him. She doesn't want any more unnecessary drama with her father's heart condition. The last thing she needs is for him to have a heart attack; maybe she had better not mention it at all but wait until her father is away on a business trip or holiday to act on what she is hearing at night. They entertain the day without Michelle saying a word about the intruder. Steven goes home again after dinner.

Each night Michelle hears the intruder in the kitchen; she wonders why the maid doesn't realize food is going missing. After a few weeks of the intruder Michelle has lost all fear she had of the stranger. She is still unsure of whether to mention it or not; so she continues to stay quiet about it.

Another few weeks pass and Michelle's visit to the fracture clinic is a happy one; she can finally weight bear on her arm. The bone has fully healed and she just needs to wait for the foot. The Doctor x-rays the foot and the bone has healed enough for Michelle to wear a boot especially designed for broken bones in the foot. The boot is fitted and she is given crutches as well to help her walk. She is so happy to be out of the wheelchair and have her independence back; although she is not quite as happy as Steven is with the result. Michelle is proud of her efforts. She gets her father to take her to the police department to check in on any new evidence. She is told that the car accident she had was not an accident at all but someone had deliberately put the oil on the road immediately before she drove out her drive way. The oil was not engine oil but ordinary cooking oil bought from a shopping center; the bottle was found only meters away from the spill; also the spill was contained and had not spread a great distance, making the accident suspicious. Unfortunately the oil bottle was wiped clean and therefore there are no finger prints to examine. Michelle spots Lola in the station and walks over to say hello "So what are you doing in the station?" asks Michelle.

"Well I became so intrigued at witnessing the fire starter run from the house across the road, I've decided I'd like to become a Detective so I've volunteered to help here at the station."

"What have they got you doing?"

"Just errands; vacuuming, mopping, going out to buy doughnuts and coffee, things like that."

"Well when I get back I'll see if I can get you to help on the case; but you will have to swear to secrecy; okay?

"Not a problem."

"What about your parents; what do they think?"

"They now know I saw someone running away from the fire so think it's great I want to help; they are so proud of me, I didn't even get into trouble."

"That's great news but I'd better be going before Steven comes looking for me. I'll see you soon."

"Bye!" Sure enough on her way out the door Steven is just coming in. The family drive back to the estate, thrilled with the good result today. They do nothing else for the day but relax and have an early dinner and decide on an early night. The day has made them tired with the trip to Los Angeles.

Susan and Steven finally get some time alone together on the estate; but Susan still won't leave the estate for a date until Michelle is completely healed. Michelle is secretly happy about this decision of Susan and supports her one hundred percent; Steven is not so happy but goes along with it to keep Susan happy. He knows Michelle does not like him or trust him; he just doesn't understand why.

Michelle has another visit with the doctor; it's been ten weeks since the break. He x-rays the foot and tells Michelle her bone is strong enough for the boot to come off but she must not return to work for two more weeks. She still needs to rest the foot as much as possible, slowly introducing more and more weight bearing until she can use it as normal without any pain. Christopher insists she still stay at his house until she can return to work; Michelle doesn't fight the decision. They return home and the first thing Michelle does is go for a swim. She then sits with her foot raised for the afternoon. By bedtime Michelle is exhausted and sleeps the whole night without waking to the sounds of the intruder.

The next week while Steven is away the sisters go wedding dress shopping. Susan feels each dress and tries them on; Michelle takes photos of her to help her decide what she wants. She doesn't choose one that day but instead waits for the photos to be developed so she can feel which one she likes best. Michelle helps her with description of the color and design of the dress as best she can and gives her opinion on what suited her best. Susan decides it is way too early to purchase a dress but can take her time to decide; after all the day was fun and with new styles out early next year, she can do it all again.

It is Michelle's last day in the mansion and Steven is away flying. After a day of just relaxing with her father and Susan she goes to bed early to be ready for tomorrow. That night she awakes again to the intruder and gets out of bed and opens her door, narrowly. She can see a male figure in the kitchen. The man looks like Steven; but how can that be when he is meant to be away flying? She decides to visit his house tomorrow.

Chapter Twenty-Two

Michelle is up early and drives to the house her father showed her. She arrives about eight am before Steven has the chance to leave. She rings the door bell and is greeted by an elderly lady. "Good morning; I'm Detective Michelle Walker from Los Angeles," says Michelle introducing herself while showing her badge. The lady gets a worried look on her face, Michelle quickly says "Its okay, I haven't come with bad news." The lady lets out a relief sigh. Michelle adds "I'd like to speak with Steven Sheppard; is he home?"

"Steven died about two years ago," the old lady replies with tears and a croaky throat.

"Oh; please forgive me I had no idea, I'm sorry I must have the wrong Steven," Michelle says and turns to leave the lady before her.

"Detective, wait; please tell me more, I want to know more; come inside." Michelle accepts the invitation and enters the house. Mrs Sheppard takes Michelle to the living area, she picks up a photo of Steven and shows it to Michelle. "Is this the Steven you are looking for?" She requests of Michelle. Michelle takes the photo in her hands and has a good look at the man pictured before her. It is definitely another man. "No, I'm sorry it's not him," she hands the photo back to Mrs Sheppard. "Please tell me why you have come here to look for this particular Steven Sheppard?" Mrs Sheppard asks of Michelle.

"Before I answer that will you tell me how your son died?"

"Well he had a car accident and he was dead on impact, I had to I.D. his body," she tells Michelle while crying throughout the answer. Michelle puts her arms around her to comfort her. "I'm so sorry this is upsetting you so, maybe it is best if I just leave."

"No Detective, I want to know more. You see, my son was a mechanic and the forensics said he had his accident due to a mechanical fault. I find that hard to believe; I'm sure my son met with foul play, but the police here won't agree."

"What sort of mechanical fault?"

"He had his tires bald, all of them. I know my Steven and he wouldn't have driven with bald tires. He got into his car from work; it was raining and his car had no traction and he slid across the road into an oncoming car."

"So therefore the police put the accident down to his tires. Was anyone else injured or killed?"

"No; luckily the driver of the other car just got away with a broken arm. Please Detective help me, I believe someone killed Steven. Now why are you looking for this other Steven?"

"This other Steven dates my sister and she first met him because his car broke down outside the front of my father's house and this is the house my father dropped him back to. He said he lived here."

"How long ago was that?"

"Nearly two years ago."

"Detective do you think it's possible that this Steven killed my Steven and stole his identity? Steven's wallet was never found at the scene of the accident."

"Well I wouldn't like to speculate, but I'll investigate this further and get back to you. You must keep this to yourself though, you cannot tell not even one person because if your son did meet with foul play as you say and the killer finds out you suspect, your life will be in danger. Can you promise me that?"

"Yes Detective, can I have your number?"

"I'll take your number and if I find anything I'll contact you; it'll be safer that way."

"Yes of course Detective." Michelle pulls out her note pad and writes her number down. Michelle thanks the lady for her time and leaves. This new information has her intrigued. Did Susan's Steven kill this Steven and steal his identity as Mrs Sheppard says and if so Susan is in danger. Is Steven the reason for all the bad that has taken place on her family and if Steven isn't Steven; then who is he?

Michelle heads back to Los Angeles and goes to the station. Nothing has changed, still the same photos, no new evidence. She talks to the Sheriff and asks can she involve Lola in the investigation. She is told no. She tells Lola the news but also tells Lola she has her own investigation she is working on if she'd like to help with that. Lola of course jumps at the opportunity and accepts the invitation. Michelle goes about her day as normal. On her way home she decides to stop at the Belief Church to see how Minister Davis is doing with his trying to reopen the orphanage. As she walks in she spots her father inside talking with Minister Davis. She quickly hides behind the wall of the open door, realizing they did not notice her; she listens to the conversation.

"I am a financial member of this church and I therefore expect to know where the church is at financially and how far off another orphanage is," Christopher states with quite a tone to his voice. Michelle hears a couple of footsteps walking toward the desk inside the room, followed by a big bang. Has her father just punched the desk, she wonders? Next she hears a gulp followed by "Yes Christopher of course, but you haven't dedicated any time here."

"Don't you call me Christopher, you address me by my real name and we both know why I'm not allowed to dedicate time here, don't we?"

"Yes Christopher," answers Minister Davis with fear in his voice.

"I said call me by my real name, now do so."

"Yes Ugnè." Michelle lets out a slight gasp and leaves before she is heard or seen.

Back at her apartment, Michelle feels she has to warn Susan of the danger she is in and dials her father's number. Susan picks up the phone and in a shaky voice Michelle says "Susan is everything ok?"

"Yes; why's that is everything okay with you?"

"Yes I'm okay are you home alone?"

"Yes; just me, Molly and the maid, why's that? Michelle you sound scared what's wrong?"

"I can't tell you over the phone I need to speak to you in person."

"At least tell me what it's about."

"Say nothing to anyone and don't marry Steven just yet but it's about our father. I'll pick you up next Tuesday on my day off and tell you everything I know in person."

"Okay; but why should I put off marrying Steven if this is about Dad?"

"I'll explain everything when I see you, until then act normal and don't tell Dad I phoned; okay?"

"Okay!"

"I love you Susan."

"I love you too Shell, see you Tuesday." Susan hangs up the phone very confused with the conversation she just had.

It's Friday and the police are at another crime scene, this time its Michelle's place. She didn't show up for work and didn't call in sick. Her partner Donna called in to see if she is okay and found Michelle dead on her living room floor. Her head has been severely burnt and she has the letter U branded on her stomach. The police take this as the killers' calling card. She was obviously burnt elsewhere and bought back to her apartment as there is no signs of fire damage in the apartment. Someone has to notify her father and Susan; Donna being Michelle's partner offers to go. The Sheriff goes with her.

Chapter Twenty-Three

Christopher answers the door; he stands before Donna with a worried expression on his face. Somehow deep inside he already knows the horrible words he is about to hear. Donna never shows up with the Sheriff and not Michelle. He collapses to the floor weeping and shaking; this gets Susan's attention and immediately she goes to her father, embracing him but not knowing why. "Daddy, Daddy; what's wrong? Who's there?" she asks facing the open door. "Susan it's me; Donna."

"What's wrong, why is Daddy so upset?" suddenly the answer dawns on Susan as she also breaks into a weeping sorrowful cry. Donna immediately enters the house and embraces the father and daughter of her partner. "Why Michelle? How, what happened to her?" Christopher asks through his sobs. By now Donna is also a weeping mess so the Sheriff with a creaky voice says "Michelle has been murdered." Susan lets out a horrific scream and grabs her father tighter. Molly is whining at Susan's feet, sensing something is wrong. "Murdered! How was she murdered?" Christopher asks among his sobs.

"Mr Walker the details are shocking, are you sure you want that answered now?"

"Yes!" Christopher raises to his feet and invites the police into the sitting room where he can settle and have his questions answered. The group all walk into the sitting room to experience the most awkward moment in their lives. "Tell us exactly what happened to Michelle and don't leave a thing out no matter how bad this is. Susan do you want to stay and hear or would you prefer not know?" Christopher asks

"I will stay," is the simple answer Susan gives.

The Sheriff clears his throat and says "Michelle didn't arrive for work this morning and didn't call in sick, which is most unlike her so I sent Donna to go check on her. When Donna got to her apartment her door was obviously broken and ajar and Donna found Michelle on the living room floor. She knew immediately that Michelle was dead and phoned the department to report the murder."

"How did she know immediately she was dead?" asks Christopher

"Well Mr. Walker the details are horrific."

"Tell me; just tell me, I want to know everything."

"Michelle's head had been severely burnt. She was dead." Susan lets out a mournful gasp.

"Just her head? What about her body?"

"Just her head; her body has bruises of being bound. We believe she was murdered elsewhere and then taken back to her apartment to be found."

"So the killer wanted her to be found?"

"Yes, so it would seem."

"But why; does he want to be found? Did he leave any clues? Was the apartment trashed or anything stolen?"

"No the apartment wasn't trashed and nothing was stolen, not even Michelle's wallet. We do believe however that the killer was looking for something although we cannot imagine what it is. We know her phone line had been tapped, there's evidence of that. Our team are investigating as we speak, asking the neighbors did they witness anything or hear anything."

"So someone has been spying on Michelle for some time?"

"It would seem so Mr Walker. The only clue left was the killer branded the letter U onto Michelle's stomach and left it exposed for us to see."

"The letter U; what is that meant to mean?"

"We don't know Mr Walker, we are investigating that too." Susan's ears prick at the sound of the letter U being branded onto Michelle. Steven has a birth mark shaped like a U. Should I say so? No not now I'll wait till we know more. She does however ask "Was Michelle already dead when she was branded?"

"We believe she was alive at the time of branding. We are waiting on autopsy results to see if she was alive when her head was burnt."

"Oh that's horrible," sobs Susan. Molly rests her chin on Susan's lap and Susan leans down and pats her.

"Anyway I've heard enough, you two can leave and get to solving this murder and you had better do it before I do or I'll be in jail for murder," Christopher states while standing and shaking hands with the Sheriff.

After consoling Christopher and Susan, the Sheriff and Donna leave. Christopher and Susan comfort each other and spend quite some time just sitting, allowing the tears to flow. They finally discuss funeral plans. Both decide that because of the way she died that they would bury her; a cremation just might satisfy this sick murders mind. They both go to the funeral home to make the arrangements. With this done Susan decides it's time to tell Steven about Michelle. She phones him and asks can he visit tonight. Steven of course says yes. That night Susan is an emotional wreck as she informs Steven of Michelle. Steven doesn't know what to say so just says sorry and hugs both Christopher and Susan so they have a shoulder to cry on.

Donna shows up on Sunday to inform Christopher and Susan that the person is definitely identified as Michelle. The DNA results were a perfect match. She also says they can have Michelle's body for burial as they won't need to keep her for further analysis. The planned funeral can go ahead.

It's the day of the funeral. Michelle is laid in a white coffin and is given just a graveside service. The family have requested just a small funeral so only Christopher, Susan, Steven, Donna and the Sheriff are there. The Sheriff keeps his eye open for any onlookers as sometimes the killer likes to watch the funeral of his/her victim. As Christopher is too distraught to talk he asks the Sheriff would he read the Eulogy. The Sheriff reads:

Michelle Anne Walker was born on October 31, 1985; first born of Christopher and Susan Walker. It was a very special Halloween for the couple. At age eight Michelle became big sister to Susan but at the same time sadly lost her Mother during this birth; making Michelle hate hospitals. It was that very day that Michelle changed forever. She took on role of big sister with great delight and loved and protected Susan so much that she also took on the role of Susan's Mother. Michelle was always a very wary person with suspicions of everyone and everything. Her becoming a crime investigator was no accident, she was eager to be a detective from a young age and fulfilled that dream as soon as she graduated from University. In her work, Michelle gave all she had to give; work became her life. She was a career minded woman who was not interested in getting involved with a man and settling down and having children. To her

Susan was not only her sister but Michelle loved Susan as a daughter and was satisfied with the life she was living. Although we will never see Michelle age she will always be with us in memory and in our hearts. She will stay forever young and beautiful.

As the coffin is lowered into the ground, Susan grabs onto Steven nearly collapsing and Christopher notices a young girl in the distance watching the funeral. He walks toward her and asks her "Did you know Michelle?"

The young girl nods her head "Yes, she was very nice to me."

"What is your name?"

"Lola"

"Hello Lola, I'm Michelle's father, Christopher. Come over with me and you can say your goodbye." Christopher takes Lola by the arm and walks her over to the burial place. On their walk he learns how Lola met Michelle and is glad she wants to follow in her footsteps. Once back to the small group Christopher takes Lola and introduces her to Susan and Steven. Lola immediately likes Susan and can understand why Michelle was so protective of her. She takes some rose petals and throws them on the coffin and says her goodbye. Christopher asks Lola to join them back at his house for some refreshments; Lola accepts the offer.

Back at the mansion, Lola is amazed. She had no idea that Michelle was part of a wealthy family; she was always so humble. Christopher likes Lola and encourages her to come visit him and Susan whenever she wants. He wants to know what Michelle saw in Lola to become protective of her as well. Lola says she will; especially now she has a licence and can drive. Lola makes the effort to talk with Susan to get to know her a bit more. Susan also likes Lola and says she would like for her to visit. She puts Lola's phone number into her cell and gives her number to Lola. After some hours Lola says she must leave and thanks Christopher for his hospitality. She leaves happy with the decision she made to watch the funeral. The Sheriff and Donna also say it's time they left. The sheriff is unhappy that he didn't spot anyone other than Lola watching the funeral. After they leave there is an unusual silence within the mansion. Christopher breaks the silence by announcing he is tired and is going to rest. Susan asks Steven would he mind leaving as she is also tired and would love to rest. The rest of the day is spent with Christopher and Susan in their rooms.

Chapter Twenty-Four

ichelle's Lawyer announces to Christopher and Susan that Michelle has only one beneficiary and that it is Susan. Christopher is most happy with this and says he will leave so the Lawyer can tell Susan in confidence. The Lawyer tells Susan that she will have to come see him at his office to inherit Michelle's estate; an appointment is arranged and the Lawyer leaves. Susan feels quite upset again.

The day has arrived for the will to be read and Susan goes to see the Lawyer. Susan takes a seat and she is told of her inheritance. She has inherited all Michelle's money, the apartment, her car, the furniture and a key. The key is for Michelle's bank safe and comes with special instructions. Nobody including Christopher is to be told that Michelle had a safety box at the bank and Susan is to listen to the CD in the safe and then decide what to do. Michelle has left instructions so that she will know what to do. The Lawyer hands the key to Susan as Susan is very confused at the knowledge of Michelle having a secret bank safe and why no one can know. Susan takes the key and puts it in her zip pocket of her purse and is also handed the keys that once belonged to Michelle for her apartment and car. Susan thanks the Lawyer and goes to see the bank. At the bank another appointment is made for Susan to open the safe as Michelle made arrangements prior to her death for Susan to be able to listen to the CD at the bank in a sound proof room.

Susan is very confused but intrigued by this secret CD that her sister has left her and waits for her appointment with anticipation. Christopher inquires of Susan what she inherited. He is told the apartment, furniture, car and money. Susan does not mention the bank safety deposit box as Michelle requested. Christopher gives his daughter a kiss on the forehead and says he is happy she was left everything. They go about their day as normal as can be.

The day has arrived for Susan to be able to listen to the CD. She arrives at the bank and is taken to the safety deposit box. Inside is a folder a key and the CD. Next Susan is taken to a sound proof room and is given ear phones and the CD is put on for her. Alone and frightened Susan listens carefully to what the CD says. On it Michelle has recorded herself talking she says:

My Dearest Susan if you are listening to this, I am no longer with you. My guess is I have been murdered and you and Daddy are devastated. You need to take your grieving time and then you must link the evidence I have gathered and find out who murdered me. Before you is a folder, which I have had all papers typed in Braille for you. I have been holding my own private investigation into the fires and I believe there is a connection between them and our father. Daddy is involved with The Belief Church and has been for many years. Why he has never informed us of this fact I do not know but I believe it is connected with the fires and possibly even my murder. I believe Daddy is unaware of this; so say nothing to no one. Take the time to read all the evidence before you and seek out help to keep investigating. Find someone you can trust and get them to help you but not Donna, the police must not know of this or they will take all evidence from you. I love you Susan.

The CD ends and Susan is crying. She has lots to read and think about. Susan changes the safety deposit box to her name and keeps the CD stored at the bank. Since she is the only one who can read Braille she takes the folder with her to read at home. Susan's head is in a spin; what did Michelle mean by their fathers unknown involvement in all the crime that has taken place? At home Susan puts the folder in her drawer and decides to read tomorrow as she spends the afternoon upset.

The next day Susan takes the folder from her drawer and begins to read. Michelle has organized the papers into sections. One section is all about The Belief Church, a section on evidence and suspects and a section on other cases and people she has met during her investigation. The first section Susan decides to read is on her father. She reads:

Christopher Walker has once been a member of The Belief Church and is still financially supporting them on a regular basis. I Michelle Walker am his daughter and have witnessed him at The Belief Church on several occasions. I have asked Daddy about his involvement with the Church but he gets angered and is very evasive. I have overheard a conversation between Daddy and Minister Davis. Minister Davis called Daddy Ugnè; this is Daddy's real name. Daddy has a birth certificate for an Ugnè Lanka from Lithuania. This birth certificate is kept in Daddy's secret library. I have researched the name Ugnè and its meaning is fire. Minister Davis said that Ugnè left the Church thirty to forty years ago and he has not heard from him since. Minister Davis seems very intimidated by Daddy. Under Daddy's house is a dungeon. I have been inside this dungeon and I am quite sure there is someone living in there. The key inside this deposit box is the key to the dungeon. Access is via a trapdoor in the bushes at the front of the house.

Susan is very intrigued by this information on her father. The next section she reads is on The Belief Church. She reads:

The Belief Church is a very wealthy church with an estimated wealth of several billion dollars. The church is unusual in the way in which it operates. The people of the church are so dedicated it's as if they belong to the church and cannot leave once a member. Nobody attends a service as all service is inside the church itself. The members financially support the church and volunteer to keep the Orphanage running and the church operational. Members of the church live in the community without citizens even knowing they are members. *Susan concludes it might be why her father never took them to the church.* I have had access to the church computer which the password oddly enough is Ugnè. In the computer is an unnamed file which requires a different password which I do not know and haven't cracked as yet. The Belief Church is very unusual and isn't common, in fact it's the only one I can find in the world. *Susan reads through The Belief Church Newsletters that Michelle has had typed for her.*

Susan finds this information weird but thinks it is important to the investigation. She decides to read the section on people Michelle has met during her investigation. She reads:

I have met a young girl by the name of Lola. She was witness to the fire of the Lawyer's house; Mr Peter and Mrs. Shirley Bradford. She has become interested in becoming a Detective and has started work volunteering at the Station. I feel I can trust her and have taken her under my wing. I like Lola she is a nice girl who is very cooperative. I have also met a Mrs. Sheppard. She had a son by the name of Steven who died around the same time that Steven met Susan. Mrs. Sheppard lives in the house Steven got Daddy to drop him to on the first night Daddy met him.

Susan is happy Michelle took Lola under her wing and realizing her sister has a good judge of character decides if Michelle can trust her that she can too.

Next Susan takes the section on other cases and reads:

So far we have two cases; the Bradford's house and The Belief Church Orphanage burning down. I personally also believe Susan's car accident and bashing, Steven's bashing and my car accident are all connected to the arsonist. The arsonist seems to have some kind of vendetta on our family. *Susan didn't connect the misfortunes of her family to the arsonist cases but now with Michelle dying in the horrific way she did, maybe she is on to something.* In 1981 on January fifth, a Wendy Summers disappeared and an Ugnè Lanka also disappeared two days later on January seventh. I know Daddy is Ugnè, but where is Wendy Summers? Are these two disappearances connected? *Susan reads the enclosed Newspaper articles Michelle has had typed for her.*

Susan takes the final section of suspects and evidence and reads through them. She reads:

<u>Minister Davis</u>

- Denied knowledge of Ugnè.
- Uncooperative with investigation.
- Secret file on computer.

<u>Christopher Walker</u>

- Denied having connection with The Belief Church.
- Not only upset over Orphanage burning down, but was sorry (repeatedly).

Steven Sheppard

- Looks match witness' description.
- Drives a car hired out to a Mr Joseph Bradford – who disappeared about same time as Steven appearing.
- Steven's threat to me – and I quote 'the forgiveness is for Susan's benefit only, never make the same mistake of blaming me again or else.' Daddy saw this on our home camera system and also knows of the threat.

Susan starts to cry as she reads the evidence against her own father and fiancée. She sits for some time to recover and puts the folder back in her drawer.

Chapter Twenty-Five

Steven is once again visiting; Susan with this new knowledge has to act exactly the same so as not to give any warning that she is now suspicious of him herself. Steven asks "would you like to have a picnic on the grounds?"

Susan declines telling him "I'm still too upset over Michelle to have fun."

"Okay, I guess fun can wait, although the longer you morn the longer it will take to feel normal again and to not morn life has to get back to normal." Just at that moment Christopher enters the room and overhears what Steven has said. "Yes my darling Susan, Steven is right; you must not mope around the house any longer it's time to start living again. It's a beautiful day; why don't the two of you go and enjoy yourself?"

"Where do you suggest, Sir?"

"The amusement park, Susan hasn't been in years."

"Daddy it's hardly the place for a blind girl."

"Nonsense! Leave Molly here and let Steven be your guide. The rides will be fun without sight."

"Leave Molly; I've never left her, I don't know if I can."

"I will look after her, you two go have fun." With reluctance, Susan does as her father says. She walks out the house unhappy.

They arrive at the amusement park and Steven opens Susan's door for her and guides her to the front gates. Once inside the park Susan can hear all the music and the sound of people talking all around her. It is quite a daunting experience; she has never been anywhere so busy since being blind. Steven asks "What ride would you like to ride?"

"Well I'm here so I might as ride them all." Steven takes her to the first ride he sees and buys two tickets. They get strapped in and up they go, high in the sky. The ride spins them and turns them upside down. Susan asks Steven to close his eyes and experience the ride the same as her. He does so and he likes it. The ride is over and they both get off a bit giddy on their feet. To Susan's surprise she had lots of fun and can't wait for the next ride. They have ride after ride until Steven says he has had enough. He takes Susan to a cafe` within the amusement park and they order lunch. Over lunch Susan tells Steven that he was right and she needed to do something. Getting out of the house for the day was the best medicine for her. After lunch they visit the animal pavilion. This is definitely different for Susan. She cannot see the animal but has fun guessing by patting the animal. Sometimes the animal gives a noisy clue, making her guess easy. Steven enjoys watching the expressions on Susan's face. He is amazed how such simple things in life can bring one such joy. After quite some time with the animals, Susan wants to ride again. Steven has had enough of rides by now but goes riding again. After several rides Steven is feeling quite ill and wants to leave. Susan teases him how a blind girl can outride him but allows them to leave. On the way back to the car Steven takes Susan by the hand; she can feel his U shaped birthmark. Suddenly it dawns on her that the U is on the right wrist instead of the left. How can a birthmark suddenly change its position on the body? It can't! Susan does not say anything but is suddenly frightened. Is this person an imposter? The ride home is in silence as Susan's mind is full of questions and worries over the birth mark.

At home Molly comes racing to the car to greet Susan. She is very excited, jumping all over Susan. She runs away to the bush out the front of the house and Susan calls her back. She sniffs Steven and starts to growl. Susan tells her to stop and the growling adds to her suspicion of Steven. Why would Molly suddenly growl at Steven? Molly again leaves Susan and runs to the bush. Steven takes Susan by the hand and leads her up the steps onto the veranda. Together they sit in the swing holding hands and talking about how much fun they had at the park. Steven finally says it's time he must leave and gives Susan a kiss. Somehow the kiss feels different to Susan. Steven leaves and Susan is left feeling confused about the U, Molly's reaction and now the kiss. Susan spends the afternoon researching the papers Michelle left for her. She adds the three strange things about Steven to his evidence list.

The next day Steven is away flying so Susan decides to get in touch with Lola. She rings and Lola says she needs to stay home all day but Susan can visit at her house. Susan gets the chauffeur to take her to Lola's. The day begins with the two women getting more comfortable with each other. Susan asks Lola to her car and then asks "So Lola did you actually get to do any detective work with Michelle?"

"No not really, Michelle tried to get me to help on the arson case but the chief wouldn't allow it. She did however tell me she had her own investigation which I could help on."

"Have you told anyone of this?"

"Only you."

"Good because Michelle has left me information on what she was investigating but I cannot involve anyone unless I can have their complete trust and confidence. Michelle wrote for me to find someone I can trust to help me and also wrote she trusts you so I figure if Michelle can trust you so can I."

"Oh you can trust me I promise. I haven't told anyone not Mum, Dad or Donna about what Michelle discussed with me."

"What did Michelle discuss with you?"

"I'm not sure you will want to know."

"You can tell me because I'm sure it's about Steven."

"Yes actually it is. Michelle didn't trust him and believes he is behind the crime."

"Yes, but that can't be so because Steven has always had an alibi when the crimes took place, plus he got bashed himself."

"I know, it just doesn't make sense."

"Do I have your absolute trust on this Lola?"

"Yes I promise."

"Well I think together we need to go through what Michelle left me. It is all in Braille so I will need to read it to you and you can take notes. I don't know where we can safely do so though because Michelle's phone was tapped and I'm worried our house may be tapped as well and possibly yours. Wherever we meet it must be in a top secret location, somewhere where it can't possibly be tapped, any ideas?"

"Maybe the Library or just the park."

"I think the park sounds best, lets meet next Tuesday; is that fine with you?"

"Sure is and I'll pick you up."

"Okay Lola it's been good to speak to you until then good bye."

"Bye Susan, I'll be looking forward to working with you." Lola gets out of the car and heads back into her house. Susan gets the Chauffeur to drive her home. She feels anxious but excited at the same time; hopefully with Lola's help she can solve the case

Chapter Twenty-Six

Steven is visiting with Susan once again. Ever since the death of Michelle he feels Susan is distant from him. He decides to approach the subject of their wedding "Susan, Darling will we plan more of our wedding today?" he asks in desperation.

"No not today, I don't feel like it."

"How about the engagement party then; we haven't had one of them yet?"

"No not that either I don't feel like celebrating. We had a little party here, remember?"

"Yes, but that wasn't really a party, let's have a big one."

"I don't feel like it."

But we're getting married." At that moment Christopher enters the room.

"Married; yes you are indeed. We need to start organizing another engagement party."

"Daddy I was just telling Steven I don't feel like celebrating. Besides we already celebrated the engagement."

"No not yet, not properly we haven't. That celebration was just you, Steve, a few guests, Michelle and I, let's celebrate properly invite all family and friends."

"But I don't feel like it."

No Darling I know, but that doesn't mean we can't organise the party for the future; get things under way," responds Christopher.

"I agree totally, Sir," injects Steven.

"Yes of course; let's do this," says Christopher in his authoritative voice.

"But Daddy I don't feel like it today," Susan says thinking she is not sure she wants to go ahead with the marriage until she can eliminate Steven from the suspect list.

"Susan Darling, you will never have a day when you feel like it and the wedding will be here and nothing will be organised, so let's do this today," states Christopher. Susan breaks into a weeping cry and Christopher hugs her saying "There there, I know it's hard with Michelle not with us but the longer we put off things and getting our life back to normal the harder it will be. Have your cry and then let's organize the party and then it might make you feel better." Susan cries heavily in her father's arms. After some time she settles down and Christopher helps her back into the chair. Christopher goes off to get paper and a pen to write down the plan and guest list. "Let's start with the kind of party you want," states Christopher, he adds "Do you want a sit down affair, canapé's, buffet or a barbeque dinner?"

"Susan which would you like?" Steven asks.

"Just something simple, nothing fancy," she answers.

"So a barbeque it is then," announces Christopher, as he writes it down. "Now for, entertainment; let's think about that," he adds "How about a country theme?"

"I like it," answers Steven.

"Yes I think so," says Christopher "We can place hay bales for people to sit on and have a hay ride with the horse and wagon. We can also play country songs or have a live band that plays country."

"I really like it, what do you think Susan?" asks Steven. Susan just nods her head, having no verbal input.

"Righto that's settled then," Christopher states also writing down the theme. "Now I'll leave you two to do up the guests list," he says handing Steven the paper to write down the list. Susan gives Steven all the names for her guests and asks who he would like to invite. He replies "Nobody."

"Nobody at all?" asks Susan, quite shocked at the response. "Surely there must be someone, a family member, a work colleague or a friend; someone"

"No, nobody; just your family and friends are all I need there."

"Well okay if you say so," answers Susan; secretly suspicious as to why he has nobody to invite, not even one person.

"Now that's done what else would you like to do today Susan?"

"Nothing else just sit around here and relax." Steven accepts the answer and agrees to do whatever Susan wants.

Meanwhile in the dungeon a man unknown is listening in to every word spoken. This man has a hostage, a female hostage. Her name is Michelle; she is not dead after all and she has just heard all the conversations of the house above. She looks at the man and asks his name; he does not answer. He looks just like Steven; she demands she tell her his name and where he came from. The man still refuses to answers. Michelle cannot get away, not because she is tied because she isn't but the man has a gun and Michelle knows that nobody in the house can hear anything from within the dungeon. Also Michelle realizes only her father has knowledge of the dungeon. Does her father know about the man living down here? Michelle does not know the answer to this question. All day Michelle asks the man to speak to her and tell her how long she has been down there. All day the man ignores Michelle. All Michelle can do is advise a plan to escape; but how?

Upstairs after a day of doing literally nothing Susan tells Steven she would like him to leave but assures him the next time she sees him she might be in a better mood. Steven suggests if Susan doesn't start feeling happier soon that she see her doctor; Susan is not happy with this suggestion and shows Steven by not even acknowledging him with an answer. Steven sensing Susan is displeased with him says goodbye and leaves without even giving her a cuddle. Susan tells him to ring before visiting again to see if she is up to it; Steven leaves very worried. He drives out the driveway down the road to an alcove half a mile up the road, parks the car and walks back to the mansion. He unlocks the trapdoor under the bush and lets himself into the dungeon.

Inside the dungeon Steven is surprised to see Michelle awake and questioning the unknown man. Michelle is more shocked to see Steven and cries "Steven thank goodness you found me please help me; this man has me hostage." Steven looks at Michelle and laughs, Michelle suddenly becomes aware that Steven is not here to help her and becomes very frightened. As she looks at both men together she realizes they must be twins. Steven satisfies her query with "Michelle I see you met my twin brother."

"Who are you Steven, what are you doing?"

"I am your worst nightmare come to life and what I am doing is not to be revealed to you just yet."

"What is your brother's name and how long have you lived down here?"

"My brother's name is U; that is just the letter U and I have lived here before I met you."

"Why? What is your plan?"

"More questions you don't need to know yet."

"You have my family believing I am dead, why?"

"Yet again another question I cannot answer."

"You're responsible for all the bad things that have gone on, aren't you and of course you always had the perfect alibi while your brother did everything."

"Well it looks like the detective in you is still at work."

"Why Steven, why?"

"In time Michelle, you will find out in time."

"You won't get away with this."

"I already have. Are you hungry?"

"Yes I am."

"U, bring some food and the chains." U takes the food and chains to Steven. Steven chains Michelle and gives her some food. "We can't have you escaping now, can we? We know you know all about this dungeon." Michelle takes the food and eats. "Anyway that's enough for tonight." Steven and U leave Michelle in the room and go to their own rooms.

Chapter Twenty-Seven

Susan gets ready for Lola to pick her up; she has her papers ready to go through with Lola to see if they can together get any closer to solving the case. Lola arrives and they leave and head to the city park where there are lots of people. It's a beautiful day; the sun is shining as Lola looks around at all the park has to offer; beautiful trees bushes with flowers and grass so green. She looks at Susan and feels a sudden sadness for her. Susan reads to Lola the evidence Michelle has collected so far. . Susan says "I feel there must be some connection between the three suspects but what?"

Lola answers "I really don't know, we have to be missing something."

"I wonder if Mrs. Sheppard can help us with any information? I will get Steven to tell me where he lives and drive me to his house so we know where she lives. If Mrs. Sheppard lives there and Steven's mother is dead, where does Steven live?"

"You be careful doing that Susan; it could be dangerous."

"I'll tell him I want you to come so you will know where to visit."

"When will you do this?"

"Today, but first take me to my bank and I'll put these papers in my safety deposit box."

Lola and Susan head back to Lola's car and go to the bank and return to the park. Susan rings Steven and he comes to meet the two ladies at the park. He finds them sitting on the fountain edge, both ladies running their hands through the water. He walks over and gives Susan a kiss on the cheek and thanks her for inviting him to join them. Susan suggests they go for a walk to find a tap to give Molly a drink and passes Steven her water bowl. Steven takes Susan by the hand and the three walk side by side. "You couldn't have picked a better day for the park," Steven says taking a look at the sky above.

"Yes I can feel the warmth of the sun and my memories help me appreciate the day we have." They arrive at the tap and Steven gives Molly her water. "Steven, I've been thinking about our wedding," Susan says as Steven's face lights up with a smile. "I'd like to know where we are going to live can you take me and Lola to your house and show me, Lola can describe it to me." Steven's smile drops off his face; Lola notices but pretends she doesn't.

"I don't know if that's a good idea," says Steven

"But why? I want to know," responds Susan

"Well my house is a bit messy at the moment and I'm embarrassed."

"That's okay we don't need to go inside just take us so Lola knows where she can visit us and describe it to me; plus I have my camera so we can take a picture and I can feel what it looks like. Oh Steven I'm so excited." Unwillingly Steven walks the ladies to his car and drives them to the house.

As Steven pulls up outside the house Lola takes a good look around her to remember exactly where they are. Steven takes the camera and takes a photo for Susan. Susan hands Lola the camera to check it is a good photo. The house is of middle class, humble in design. It is painted lemon and white with a veranda along the front. As Lola is describing the house a car pulls into the driveway and an elderly lady gets out and goes to the front door and lets herself into the house. "Who is the lady going into your house, Steven?" asks Lola innocently.

"She is the cleaning lady I told you the house was a mess. We'd better go now or she will think I am checking on her," he answers quite abruptly. Susan wonders about the fear she can hear in his voice. "Anyway I'm looking at buying a house in the country, close to your father's house for us, so don't take this house seriously."

"You don't have to buy a new house Steven; I'm happy to live here."

"No I want to, somewhere with land for Molly."

"Well if you insist; I would feel safer in the country as well. Oh well Lola it looks like you won't have to remember where to visit me in town but out in the country." Steven is happy once again with this comment. "Maybe we can all look together, that would be fun," adds Susan.

"I'd like just you and me if that's okay?" Steven says in a meaningful voice.

"Well okay Darling, whatever you want," Susan says to keep Steven calm. Steven keeps driving until they are back at the park. "What say we all eat lunch together?" suggests Steven.

"That would be nice, I feel like McDonald's," says Susan

"McDonald's it is then says Steven and he drives them to the closest McDonald's restaurant. They all eat together and Steven once again drives to the park so Lola can get her car. "Thanks for the enjoyable morning Lola," says Susan.

"You're welcome; we'll have to do this again another day."

"Yes I agree; I'll text you," Susan answers and Lola gives her a cuddle goodbye and goes to her own car. Steven takes Susan home and is happy she is in a better mood today. Maybe she doesn't have depression after all, she just must have had a down day.

Chapter Twenty-Eight

In the dungeon Michelle is sick of seeing brick walls. She complains to Steven and U, but neither care. "I want to know what your plan is for me!" Michelle says quite crankily.

"When the time is right, you will know," answers Steven

"What's wrong with your brother can't he talk?"

"I can talk; when I want to that is," U says sharply. Michelle is surprised at how much he sounds like Steven; so much so that you can't tell their voices apart.

"Why did you pretend to kill me and who did you kill to make my family think it is me?"

"More questions that can't be answered," responds Steven. "Give some time and all your questions will be answered, you will know everything."

"You will never get away with this."

"I already am and will because I have the perfect plan."

"There is no such thing as a perfect plan," Michelle bluntly responds.

"You'll see, you'll see," Steven says confidently. "Any way I don't have time to talk to you about details you cannot know, I have a date with the beautiful Susan. U, see she doesn't cause any trouble. I'll see you both tonight." With that statement Steven leaves the dungeon and goes to his car to visit Susan.

Steven knocks on the door and Christopher answers. "Susan won't be long she's still in her room, come in and we'll talk." Steven follows Christopher to the sitting room. Christopher pulls out the family photo album and shows Steven the photos of Susan as a child. "Maybe some of these will be good for a slide show at your engagement party," Christopher states, he adds "You could dig out some of your childhood photos and we'll get photos also of you two dating to add to tell the romantic story."

"I only have a couple of photos of myself as a child Sir."

"That's okay, at least we have them."

"Um okay when do you want them by?"

"Well the sooner the better." Steven nods his head and thinks about which photos he will allow. Just then Susan arrives, looking as beautiful as ever.

"So where are you two off to today?" asks Christopher

"We're going to try ice skating and then enjoy a picnic at the park, Daddy."

"Well have fun."

"Daddy won't you join us?"

"Me ice skate, you have got to be kidding?"

"Well you don't have to skate but you could take some photos to add to our slideshow for the engagement party."

"Yes alright I will join you; I'll just grab the camera." Christopher leaves the room to get the camera.

Susan turns to Steven and says "I hope you don't mind I invited Daddy?"

"No that's okay," Steven answers but wishing she hadn't. Susan is happy as she really does not want to spend time alone with Steven today. She is having a difficult time with this trust issue with her new knowledge of him. Christopher returns and they all leave.

At the skating rink Steven leads Susan onto the ice and she skates beautifully. Skating is something she did often as a child and she loves being on the ice again. Around and around the rink they skate arm in arm as Christopher takes photos from the seating area. After what seems like hours they finally return to Christopher and remove their skates. Christopher snapped several good photos and shows them to Steven. He is happy with them and is actually glad Susan invited her father along. All the skating has worked Steven and Susan up a good appetite, so they are both happy to go to the park for the picnic. Christopher takes more photos at the park. Molly gets to have a run and the family relax for over an hour just lying on the blanket and talking small talk about nothing in particular. Before long three pm arrives and Steven says it's time they head home. Christopher agrees and is on his feet in an instant. The day was pleasant and Christopher is happy to see his daughter having fun and not feeling sad over Michelle. He is glad he decided to join them for the day. Steven drives them home and is asked to join them for the evening meal; he accepts the offer.

Once again the meal is eaten is silence and Steven decides he will asks Susan why this is when they are alone, as he finds it most unusual. Christopher is extremely tired from his day out and announces he is going to have an early night and tells Susan not to stay up too late. Susan and Steven go and sit on the veranda swing and spend a couple of hours there just talking and sitting. Steven takes the opportunity to ask the puzzling question about the silent eating. He says "Susan, I've noticed at meal times nobody does any talking; why is this?"

"Daddy can't stand the talking or noisy atmosphere at meals. When he was a child he was sent to war and all the men in the camp were very loud at meals and it was a violent time as food was in short supply and the men would argue over the meal with each other.

Meal time terrified Daddy and to this day he can't stand noise while eating. I think it brings back bad memories for him."

"War; your father was sent to war as a boy?"

"Yes, but not as you are thinking. He didn't have to fight but he was sent to cook for the soldiers and wash and things like that. He saw some horrible things and will never speak of it, so don't ever mention it. I think he went through a lot worse than we know."

"Yes of course, don't worry he will never know I know."

"Well I suppose I'd better go, I have to fly tomorrow. I will see you in five days when I return; what would you like to do then?"

"Um not sure, but I'll work something out before then and let you know when I see you." Steven leans in and gives Susan a kiss goodnight and heads down the steps to his car. He drives to the alcove and parks and walks the distance back and goes back into the dungeon.

The next day Steven sits around the dungeon all day. "You liar, you are not a pilot are you?" Michelle yells at him.

"Of course I'm not but I had to tell Susan I was something and a pilot suits the situation nicely."

"You don't work at all, do you?"

"You would be correct."

"How do you have money then?"

"I'm a very wealthy man, I don't need to work. That's all you need to know on the subject."

Michelle sits and ponders on this new information.

"Well knowing about Christopher's childhood days has answered some questions for me," Says Steven.

"What do you mean?" demands Michelle.

"In time, you will find out in time." Michelle is sick of having *in time* as her answer for her questions. Knowing she will not get any information, Michelle spends the days in mostly silence. She is living a miserable existence.

Chapter Twenty-Nine

Susan phones Lola and says she would like to meet with her. Lola says she is on her way. Knowing they can't talk at the house they both head off in Lola's car. They go to the Library where they can talk quietly together. Susan tells Lola she wants to visit Mrs. Sheppard, so they leave the Library and Lola drives them to the house. Knocking on the door is quite scary as they don't know what to expect. An elderly friendly lady answers and asks can she help them. Susan answers with "I certainly hope so. My sister Michelle came and saw you some months ago."

"Yes I remember her; please come in." Both ladies enter the house as well as Molly. Lola takes Susan by the hand and follows Mrs. Sheppard into her cozy lounge room. "Is there anything I can get you ladies, a cup of tea perhaps?"

"No thank you we just want to talk, if that's alright?" answers Susan.

"Yes that's fine."

Susan starts the conversation "Michelle visited you thinking she was coming to see Steven Sheppard, is that right?"

"Yes that's correct; but my Steven is dead. I believe this Steven has stolen his identity."

"Well this Steven is my fiancé and I also have doubts about him recently. My sister Michelle is now also dead."

"Oh how horrible, I'm so sorry Dear; what happened?"

"She was murdered and Michelle was secretly holding her own investigation, which is why she visited you and she suspected Steven as a suspect in the fires and some deaths. That is why we need to speak with you today. Can we see a photo of your Steven please?"

"Yes indeed." Mrs. Sheppard walks to the side board and gets the most recent photo of her Steven and hands it to Lola.

Lola says "Susan he looks nothing like your Steven, he definitely isn't the same man."

"You say your Steven said he lives here?" asks Mrs. Sheppard.

"Yes that is what he claims."

"Well I wonder where he does really live then?" Mrs. Sheppard asks, very puzzled.

"More to the point, who actually is he? It's quite scary to be engaged to a fraud."

"Yes I can imagine it would be. Do you think you can call off the engagement?"

"No I need to pretend I don't know anything in case he is dangerous."

"Oh yes, of course."

There is an eerie silence for a few minutes as Susan's mind is impounded with questions upon questions. A tear rolls down her cheek and as she rubs it off, both Mrs. Sheppard and Lola notice.

"What evidence have you got so far?" asks Mrs. Sheppard

"Well he claims he is Steven Sheppard and a pilot. He has not long turned thirty-four and says he lives here."

"Well he is the same age as my son."

"Well he would be if he stole your son's identity. But why would he do that?"

"Michelle told me when he came into your life and it was only a few weeks after Steven was killed. There has to be a connection."

"He hires a car, which he pretends to own; but the car is hired to a Joseph Bradford."

"Maybe your Steven is really Joseph Bradford."

"That has never occurred to me, maybe you are right. Joseph Bradford's parents' house was deliberately burnt down and they were both killed but Joseph was overseas at the time and thus is not a suspect. But if he is behind the killing, why would he want to burn his own parents; it doesn't make any sense?"

"Killers often don't make sense Dear. I believe Steven was deliberately made have a car accident so he would be killed as well. I believe his identity is stolen by your Steven because Steven's wallet was never found."

"I'm really scared right now," Susan states as another tear rolls down her face. Lola hugs Susan and Molly rests her head on her lap.

"Come now Dear, don't upset yourself too much, you said Steven is unaware of your suspicions; is that right?"

Susan nods her head to answer yes.

"Well you have to stay strong and not allow Steven to get suspicions. Together we will work this out. Who else knows of this?"

"No body, just us three."

"Okay, do you want to tell anyone else, your father, Michelle's work partner or anyone?"

"No we can't. My father would go ballistic and Donna would take all our evidence collected thus far and it would be out of our control and then Steven would get suspicious if the police were questioning him."

"Well we must think of a way of proving that Steven is actually Joseph. Can you get access to his wallet to photocopy his license?"

"I'm not sure. I wouldn't be able to as I can't see but maybe we could devise a plan so Lola could do it."

"An excellent idea, but what plan? Hang on I have an idea. Once you photo copy the license you could go to the rental car company and pretend Joseph sent you to enquire about the next service or something like that."

"Yes that would be good because I would have to show some ID and I could show his at the same time and if Steven's license picture is the same as Joseph we will know he is the same man."

"Now I take sleeping tablets at night, what if I give you one to slip into Steven's drink and when he is asleep, Lola can take the photocopy of his license."

"That's a great idea and I could have a barbeque by the pool and invite Lola. That way Steven is in his board shorts and his wallet will be left on the table. He could fall asleep on a poolside lay-a-bout chair. What do you say Lola, are you up for the challenge?"

"I'm game if you are. When will you organize this barbeque?"

"The next time he returns from his flying, which is in a couple of days. I'll buy him some board shorts and we can act as if it's a belated birthday barbeque so I can surprise him, that way he can't say no. We'll have just Daddy, Steven you and me. I'll keep Daddy occupied while you go inside and photocopy the license."

"I feel quite excited, it's the most detective work I will have done," states Lola. Everyone laughs at the statement.

"Be sure to let me know the result," says Mrs. Sheppard.

"We will. Thank you for your time and ideas Mrs. Sheppard but we'd better go."

"It's been my pleasure and it'll help give me some answers over my Steven as well."

Mrs. Sheppard leads them to the door and they leave feeling a little scared but a lot excited. Lola drops Susan home and heads home awaiting the barbeque.

Chapter Thirty

It's the day for Steven to visit, Susan and Lola head to the shops first thing in the morning and buy fresh buns and food for the barbecue and also gifts for Steven including the board shorts. Back at the mansion Lola wraps the gifts and Christopher organizes the barbecue. The door knocker bangs against the heavy door, Steven has arrived; time to put their plan into action. Susan excitedly opens the door and tells Steven she has a surprise for him. She takes him out back where Steven can see a barbecue being cooked and a table with gifts. "What's going on here?" Steven asks

"We're having a belated birthday celebration for you," answers Susan.

Steven smiles, happy that Susan finally feels like celebrating, it will make it easier for their engagement party to be organized. "But Darling, I don't have a swim suit," says Steven looking at Susan dressed in her bikini.

"Oh yes you do! I took care of that, here go change," says Susan holding out the board shorts.

Steven takes the shorts and goes into the house to change. He places his wallet and keys on the table and goes to the bathroom. He comes out ready for swimming. He walks over picks Susan up and throws her into the pool and then immediately jumps in as well. Together the two play in the water. Susan asks Lola to join them. Lola also jumps in. After some time in the water, Christopher says the barbecue is ready to be eaten. They get out of the pool and Steven makes his and Susan's burger. "I'll get the drinks," says Lola. She goes inside and gets the soft drink from the fridge. She quickly grabs the sleeping pill from her purse. "Let's have a wine," says Christopher as he is already pouring the glasses.

"Okay," says Lola placing the soft drink on the table. She walks over to the wine glasses and quickly drops the pill into a glass and hands the glass to Steven. She also hands a glass to Susan and takes one for herself. Steven hands Lola the burger he has made for her. Together they sit at the table and eat and drink. After eating Susan says "Time to open the presents." They all walk to the present table and Steven opens his gifts. Christopher says "Lay on the layabouts while your stomach digest some before going swimming again." Everyone lays down.

It isn't very long when Steven starts to yawn and says he feels tired from his swim. Before long his eyes are closed and he is letting out quiet snores. Christopher takes a look at Steven and says "Well if he is sleeping, I'm all sweaty from cooking I'm going to leave you girls alone and go have a shower." Perfect timing thinks Susan, saves me from distracting him. Christopher enters the house and goes upstairs.

Time to put the plan into action and fast. Lola jumps up and goes to the table and takes Steven's license from his wallet. She enters the library and quickly photocopies it and returns the license to Steven's wallet. She puts the photocopy in her purse and returns to Susan on the pool deck. When Christopher returns, the girls are chatting away. "Is he still asleep, lets wake him, it's getting late," states Christopher upon seeing Steven. He walks over and shrugs him saying his name at the same time. Steven wakes up. "Oh forgive me, I must have been more tired than I thought."

"That's okay my boy," says Christopher "We all get tired at times. It's time you had a shower and left, it's getting late."

"Yes Sir," says Steven.

"I thank you for a good night, I'll shower at home. Good bye," says Lola and she goes inside grabs her purse and leaves. She has lots to do before they can show the photocopy to the rental car company.

Steven gets out of the shower, thanks Christopher and Susan for the wonderful surprise, and gathers his gifts and leaves. Susan gives her father a cuddle good night and says she is tired and heads to her bedroom. Christopher also goes to bed.

Back at Lola's, she is busy printing Joseph Bradford and the address of Joseph and sticking it over Steven's name on the licence and re-photocopying the license. The photocopy looks great, ready for the rental company. Now she just has to wait for Steven to go back to work.

Steven has had the best night sleep he has had for years. Therefore today he feels refreshed and is ready for some fun. He heads to see Susan to see what they can do today. He knocks on the door and Susan answers, she asks did he enjoy his party last night. "Sure did and I had the best night sleep, what can we do today?" Steven responds.

"Well I haven't given today any thought," says Susan. They decide to just stay around the house and have another swim.

Chapter Thirty- One

Steven has told Susan he has to fly again. Susan texts Lola asking her to pick her up. Together the two ladies go to the rental car business. Susan introduces herself and explains to the receptionist that Joseph would like to know when the car has to be bought back for the next service. She produces the photocopy of his license and shows it to the receptionist. The receptionist on seeing the photo gives the information to Susan. The suspicion is confirmed, Steven is indeed Joseph Bradford. Susan has a shiver run up her back with the confirmation. She and Lola are both scared. Susan thanks the receptionist and they leave.

They go to see Mrs. Sheppard to inform her of their discovery. Together they discuss what to do with the new found information. Susan says she believes now is the time to involve the police and her father and inform him of the truth about Steven. Mrs. Sheppard agrees but tells Susan that there must be more to the case yet. Susan fills Mrs. Sheppard in on all that Michelle had discovered. Mrs. Sheppard says there still must be more and asks Susan has she been inside the dungeon as yet. With knowledge that the dungeons have not been explored, the three decide to go see first the police and then Christopher together.

Back at the mansion, Christopher is in his personal library sitting at his desk when he hears knocking on the door that leads to the dungeons below. He opens the door and steps into the dungeon and is immediately given a blow to his left side of his head from U with a bass ball bat. Christopher falls to the ground, nearly unconscious. U tapes Christopher's hands behind his back with duct tape and forces him to walk to the room where Steven has Michelle held captive. With the sight of Michelle alive, Christopher lets out a huge gasp and tears form in his eyes. Hanging on the wall of the dungeon room is a horse whip, a bamboo cane and photos of a young woman and a picture of the Belief Church. In the corner of the room is a fire blazing, with a handle sticking out of the flames. Also another unknown man stands smiling with his eyes fixed on Christopher. Christopher suddenly has a look of panic as fear ravishes his whole soul with the realization of what he is about to endure.

"Welcome Christopher or should I say father?" Steven says

"I have absolutely no idea what you are talking about." Responds Christopher.

"Well I suppose you wouldn't, since you didn't know me and my twin brother even existed," turning to Michelle he adds "The perfect plan is about to be revealed."

The unknown man stands and walks over to Christopher and runs his hands over Christopher's chest and down to his manly goods. Christopher spits on the man and demands he step away. U still holding onto Christopher pushes Christopher toward the unknown man and says "Take him". The unknown man grabs Christopher and tosses him onto his stomach onto the hard concrete floor. He bends down, rolling Christopher onto his back and takes hold of Christopher's pants zip and rips it open. Christopher struggles to squirm away but the unknown man being 30 years his junior and muscle bound overpowers Christopher and strips him of his pants and underwear. Unable to watch what is about to unfold, Michelle closes her eyes and hangs her head. With the sound of Christopher screaming, Michelle realizes her father is being brutally raped by this huge man.

When the screams subdue, Michelle opens her eyes and sees her father lying face down with severe scratch marks covering his back. A single tear falls from her right eye. She turns to Steven and says "Why Steven, why?"

"You want to know why, ask our father."

"What do you mean our father?"

"That's right Michelle, we share the same father." Michelle turns to look at her father to hopefully get the denial she is so desperately seeking. Christopher full of shame is unable to look at her. Turning back to Steven, she asks "Can you at least give the man some dignity and put his underwear back on?"

"NO, absolutely not!" Steven yells with anger clearly visible all over his face. "What dignity did he give my mother? None at all. So he will die the same way as her."

Steven walks over to the wall, taking the horse whip in his hand. U takes the bamboo cane and together they beat Christopher until his back and bottom is covered in cuts and flesh is no longer visible through the flood of blood. They roll him over, lashing him over and over. The whip and the bamboo cane cutting into his flesh forever leaving their mark. Michelle screams at them to stop, but the pleas go unanswered. Christopher too weak to scream anymore just endures the whipping silently. Finally for what seems like an eternity, the flogging stops. Christopher watching the twins from barely open eyes lets out one last scream as he sees U walking toward him with a red hot branding iron. Steven holds Christopher down as U pushes the branding iron with the letter U on it onto Christopher's stomach. Christopher's screams are deafening as Michelle who is tied and bound to a chair is unable to help.

Chapter Thirty-Two

At the police station Lola and Susan show the Sheriff all the evidence they have collected. The sheriff immediately organizes a squad to investigate the dungeon.

The squad of police drive into the Walker mansion driveway with sirens blaring.

In the dungeon Christopher has just been raped, flogged and branded. He is now at the mercy of the twins being held up by the other unknown huge man. Steven and U each have a dagger. Steven has his dagger resting on Christopher's neck and U has Christopher's penis in one hand and the dagger resting on the top of the penis where it joins to the body. "Silent everyone, one scream and Daddy here get his dick cut off followed by his head." Demands Steven.

Susan, Lola and Nancy all go inside and cannot find Christopher anywhere. Lola takes Susan by the hand and leads her to the trapdoor followed by Nancy. The police are already inside the dungeon. The flicker of flames shadow the dungeon walls and the smell of burning flesh fill the air. Slowly they creep deeper into the tunnel of the dungeon leading to the room of torture.

Molly runs from Susan to the room and stands growling at the three men holding Christopher. "FREEZE!" demands the sheriff, pointing his gun at Steven. Another eight policemen aim their pistols at the three men. "Anyone move and we will shoot to kill" adds the sheriff. As the three men stand still with realization they are defeated and the full result hoped for today will not be met, more policemen hone in and handcuff the three. Christopher falls to the floor in a heap. One of the officers removes his shirt and places it over Christopher giving him some dignity that has been totally stripped from him. Another officer unbinds Michelle and she rushes to her father and lays beside him cradling him in her arms. Lola is told to ring 911. Nancy takes Susan and leads her to her sister and father.

The three men are arrested and put into the back of police cars and driven to the station. The paramedics take Christopher and Michelle to the hospital and Lola drives Susan to the hospital.

Susan without any knowledge can only wait until she can speak with her father and sister to get some answers as to what happened but as for exactly why; all three have to await the twins trails.

About the Author

Debbie King, currently a stay a home wife, used to work in Early Childcare Centres. She is a first time Author and desires to write more books. She lives with her husband, Michael and they have three adult children. She lives in Gympie, Queensland, Australia.

CPSIA information can be obtained
at www.ICGtesting.com
Printed in the USA
LVOW04s1706180416

484152LV00017B/597/P